The Cr6 Terrorist

by K.A. Shott

The Cr6 Terrorist

ISBN 978-0-6151-5643-9

www.writeshott.com

The Cr6 Terrorist

***

perfect

"THOU HAS DEFILED THY SANCTUARIES BY THE MULTITUDE OF THINE
INIQUITIES,
BY THE INIQUITY OF THY TRAFFICK;

THEREFORE WILL I BRING FORTH A FIRE FROM THE MIDST OF THEE,
IT SHALL DEVOUR THEE,

AND I WILL BRING THEE TO ASHES UPON THE EARTH IN THE SIGHT OF ALL
THEM THAT BEHOLD THEE."
EZEKIEL 28:18

She put her hand to his neck. It was on fire. The tingling

began in the side of her head while her eyes read, "Environmental and

Health Risks Associated with the Use of Processed Incinerator Bottom

Ash in Road Construction."

Somehow, it suddenly made sense.

***

Dear Journal (or to whom it may concern),

The first time I saw him he looked like any other man, tall. Taller than me. I didn't love him then but—soon after when—one night we were left to close his leather tanning shop. It was my summer-vacation-before-starting-college-job. He told me a story in those late hours that shrunk him to my size. Then. There. Amidst chemical smell and dead flesh I knew I could never love another.

Anne

***

"Genevieve!" He cried out from his hospital bed.

He could not lift his head. She knew. He would have sat straight up like a child piercing through bad-dream membranes.

She never left. She spit-bathed while he watched—when he was awake.

Sometimes she wondered what he was thinking when his eyes lingered on her nipples, whether it was her he saw or another lover he'd had. "It's me, my love, Anne," she'd coo, stroking graying patch-hair above his ear. His eyebrows.

She'd thought he smiled, "Thanks, God, for the imagination."

She thought then kissed his lips, "Genevieve is coming, I promise."

She swore his eyes scolded.

***

"I was married. My daughter's name was Genevieve."

"Past tense," Anne—too quickly.

"Yes, past. . ."

Gene looked at nothing. Anne knew she'd said the wrong thing the wrong way. That was her style, she'd learned, through lost friends, loves, family. She even cut the pizza menu up from the joint of her summer-before-thesummerbeforecollege-job and taped it to her mirror as a motto:

"A person who speaks their mind must ride a fast horse."

She'd learned it didn't do good to apologize for the past passed but something possessed her vocal chords, "I'm sorry."

"For what?"

"For being such a bitch."

Gene took Anne's face into his hands. Slowly. Tenderly. There was nothing. She could see her own reflection in his pupils. "Don't ever say such a thing," he said.

Her own face seemed odd. Like his eyeballs were spoonbacks; her mouth—a gaping fish's popping%promising.   ***

6

Dear Anne,

Dr. Ierf forwarded your email to me. You have described some provocative associations, but I must admit to not being fully abreast of the latest research in this area. It does seem an epidemiological approach to the subject of hexavalent chromium exposure and rates of parkinsonism may be valuable, as would comparing blood or tissue concentrations of metals in afflicted patients to controls.

This issue may be of interest to Dr. Nam Keb who specializes in neurodegenerative disease research. I have forwarded your letter to him. Please let me know if you have any questions.

Best wishes,

Dr. Noswal

"FUCK!" She screamed into the pillow so that Gene wouldn't hear.

SHIT, SHIT, SHIT!

She threw the letter on the ground, took her heel and ground it

into the paper. Then she remembered:

God, I'm sorry. Please forgive me. Please help me with these feelings. I'm so hurt and frustrated AND DAMN IT!!! Oops, sorry God. PLEASE, help me! My emotions are so strong right now. I don't know what to do. Help me, please.

She hadn't known God until Gene. A sense came through her

insides—down deep to the bogswamp's shed where she'd learned to

keep. . . fierce as blackwalnutshell. . .

hell—PEACE.

Thanks God. . . for not giving up on me!

Anne picked up the letter, smoothed out the wrinkles her heal

had given and smiled;

At least they replied

Letter stacked on stacks of letters beside a twin tower of

shadows—her World Trade Centers:

they fell. it doesn't matter awfully much the SONSaBITCHES
wouldn't take the time or effort . . . Gosh darn it, sorry God. Please
forgive me, again. Again and again. I'm such a fuck-up. Shit, there I
go again. Sorry God.

To Gene, it mattered—Anne spending years. Trying.

Figuring. Nonsense getting sick by age-35 with an 'old person's'

disease and too old to have active multiple sclerotic lesionings not to

mention sides of dishes making wishlists not fitting either entrée

selection: PD & MS.

"Thanks for all your hard work, Anne."

"I haven't been able to find a way to cure you."

"You don't have to cure me. It's all part of God's plan. For me. For

you—us."

"God can cure you right?"

"If that's His will."

"I'm mad it's not his will!"

"I can tell. Will you pray with me?"

Anne begrudged giving up anger.

I hear his words. His voice seems so peaceful, so calm. How can it when I'm like a gale force. . . inside. . .

"Lord Jesus, Anne and I ask you to be with us. . ."

. . . I want to believe—Gene—he's better than me. . .

"and to let Your comfort and peace come into our hearts. Give us the

strength and courage we need to accept:

You have ALL things in your hands. Good. Bad. Pleasure. Pain.

Remind our minds that You do for us even when all we see is

wrongs.

Please, Lord, never let us forget—even Satan's most nefarious

task must first get Your permission for You are THE way Amen!"

Amen

***

"I'd like to apply for a job."

The woman behind the desk looked Anne up and down.

"You have to be able to lift more than 100 lbs."

"I'm strong."

The woman handed her an application.

> Date: perfect
> Name: Anne Whiting
> Position Applying For: Water Delivery

***

"Genevieve!"

"Shh, my love, shh. You'll be okay."

"Where is she? You promised!"

"I know, I know, she'll be here soon. Soon, my love, soon."

***

Dear Diary,

Driving home tonight was like riding that roller coasters whose
spit-mist plunged my stomach-to-throat. I must be schizophrenic,
carrying on conversations with my head:
Could what just happened have really happened?

At the stoplight I looked into the rearview mirror, pursed my lips
together and looked up my nostrils: no boogers. Teeth—clean.

What happèned?
Nothing, really.
Something?
Something FANtastic. Wonderful and. . . nothing at all.
He held my face in his hands and said, "NEVER."

OKAY!!! That was intense

NOTE: Ann-NO-E needs clutch-work. She lurched at the light's
green coming home. Take her out to the VWSHOP

The last thing I want to do right now is lift weights. . .

So get your LAZY Ass to the gym

. . . better go. Bill's gym! I've been pushing/pulling his weights since
pre-puberty.

***

Anne placed the application on the desk. Walking away—the lady called out, "I did tell you, you MUST be able to lift over 100 pounds?"

Anne looked at woman. Then around. Standing beside the dispenser: 2x5-gallon bottles—full. Anne grabbed Neck#1, then Neck#2. . . lift. . .flip. . .two globules of shimmers sat on her shoulders, "I may be small but I told you I'm strong."

The woman smiled. Anne sat the bottles down and the woman whispered, "Come in on Wednesday. I'll make sure you see the boss."

"Thanks."

A man said, "App," took the top sheet from the stack and sat—filling—Anne smiled, whispering backward, "Aren't you going to ask him if he can lift 100 pounds?"

The woman looked awkward.

Anne's uncanny knack for the wrong things at the right time. . .

no sense in apologizin'

. . . "sorry," Anne said. "Bad sense of humor."

The woman's forehead eased, "Oh, okay, I get it. Funny. Really. By the way, my name is Kim."

"Hi Kim. I'll see you. . ." Anne lowered her voice to a whisper,

". . . on Wednesday, say 10:00am."

"That'll be just fine, Anne."

They had a little secret-casted-darkened-casket; for all ships befriend such shadowmasts.

***

"So why ya' wanna be a guy?"

"I don't," Anne replied.

"Then why ya' tryin' to train like a guy?"

"Because I'm strong."

Bill laughed. He'd been in the gym biz decades.

"Seen 'em come. Seen 'em stop comin,'" he'd say to anyone—

listener.

He knew Anne's eyes. Their fierceness he'd seen but once

before at the docks—two Navy-boys boxed and one had those wicked

eyes; Bill never forgot his name.

"Hey kid, got any relations named Towsend?"

3x45s on each side of Olympus' bar: squat.

He remembered: she was 12 the first time she came.

Bar plus 5s

"No, why?"

"Just askin'"

***

"Franklin School, this is Doris."

"Hi Doris. My name is Anne Whiting. I need to speak with

Genevieve Whiting."

"Hold on, I'll call her to the office."

WAGNER. BEETHOVEN. NEWS ON NATIONAL PUBLIC RADIO,
"ANOTHER TERRORIST BOMBING IN..."

"Hello. This is Genevieve."

"Vieve?"

"What are you doing calling me?"

"Your father. . . he's. . .dying."

"Yeah right! You told me that before. You guys just won't stop will

you?"

"Wait! Please! Listen. He's in the hospital and he's calling for you.

He really is dying."

"You've lied too many times. You said he was dying years ago and he

wasn't."

Anne mumbled, "but he was."

"So says you. I have to go now. Do me a favor—DON'T contact me until he's in the GROUND!"

B<small>UZZZZZZZZZZZZZZZZZZZZ</small>

God help me, please. . .

***

"So you want to deliver water?"

Anne nodded.

"Why?"

"I need a job."

"You know you have to be able to lift 100 pounds."

"Yes, I know."

He looked her up and down. Head to toe. Everybody did.

"You sure you can do it."

She performed on cue. She was good at playing circus.

Setting the water bottles down, taking extra time and effort to show she had them absolutely under control every second they were in her hands.

"You see. My size doesn't mean I'm weak."

He smiled. She had learned, in her thirty-two years of life, men liked strong women that looked small and fragile.

"Drugs?"

"Absolutely not!" She was used to the question. "I worked hard to be strong."

"Here's the place for the physical. You come back with a clean bill and—drug test—you can start Monday."

"Great."

"Working Monday through Friday won't be a problem?"

"No sir. You'll find you'll have little or no problem with me at all. I like to work hard. I like to do a good job and I'm reliable."

"See you after the physical."

Perfect

***

RURRRURRRURRRURR. . . RURRRURRRURRRURRRURRRURRR

I hate you Ann-NO-E! I'm supposed to be at work. Not now, please, not now. Why me? What did I do to have such fucked up luck? The bus! I can still catch the 9:00am. I'll be late but not as late as I'll be FUCKING around with you! OUCH! Dammit, I thought tires were softer. Great! Now my toe hurts. I wonder if limping is bad for my back. Poor old Back. You've stood up for a lot of abuse over the years. Yep. It's hurting. I knew it. This day just keeps getting better and better. OH! There's the bus. I hate running. My toe really hurts. WAIT! Cool.
"Hey thanks for waiting."

"Anytime. I know you."

"Yeah, how?"

"Didn't you work out at Bill's place a long time ago?"

"Yeah. You?"

"Yeah. You don't remember. . . I used to have hair," he smiled and

patted his head.

"Oh shit. I remember now. You were a monster in the gym."

His smile sunbeamed.

God I hate how people change. Just look at him. Driving a bus and smiling because I remember what he used to be and can't even recognize him because of what he's become. I bet the drugs made his hair fall out. Probably not the only side-effect. I wonder if he can get it up now that he's, obviously, off them. I wonder. . . what Mr. Whiting. . . Eugene looks like naked. I shouldn't think. . . but the way

20

he looked into my eyes. . .he's so FUCKING awesome! Oh my God, I'm here. Oh shit, think other thoughts think other thoughts think other...

"See ya' later."

"Yeah, yeah, hey, say 'hi' to Bill next time you see him."

Anne watched his frown creep round.

I haven't lost my touch.

***

Dear Mrs. Whiting,

I am an occupational physician and work with Dr. Reye (to whom you sent your original correspondence). There are several Parkinson's specialists at this hospital. You can make an appointment for your husband with one of them regarding his treatment.

There is a federal agency with responsibility to look at environmental health concerns of communities, ATSDR, who may help if you are inquiring about the Hinckley community.

The cause(s) of Parkinson's disease are not well understood. Some familial risk factor seems likely and there are some people looking at pesticide exposures, toxic metals, mitochondrial toxicity, tobacco's protective effect, anti-inflammatory agents effects therapeutically, immune system effects, etc. All the research used to be focused on post-infectious effects and is broadening.

Unfortunately, I do not know about hexavalent chromium (Cr6/CrVI) neurotoxicity but here is a weblink you might find helpful:
http://www.atsdr.cdc.gov/toxprofiles/tp7.html#bookmark06

Best wishes,
Dr. Setrou

Dear Dr. Setrou,
Thank you for your referrals. Unfortunately most of the information used in the report you referred to me is now, at least, ten years old and the primary focus of neurological study was CVI (cardiovascular incidence) and not Parkinson's disease/parkinsonism or the effect on dopamine.

Two years ago, when I spoke to an agent at ATSDR, I was informed that there was no proof that ingestion of CrVI/Cr6/hexavalent chromium/sodium dichromate had ANY deleterious effect. I was assured that only a VERY small percentage of people were toxically exposed due to occupational exposure.

I don't, therefore, hold much hope that this agency will be helpful considering that in New Jersey, alone, there are over 160 sites deemed—by the EPA—clean-up priorities due to hexavalent chromium contamination. In fact, one county in particular (Hudson) has levels of hexavalent chromium contamination significantly greater than those at Hinckley.

Sincerely,
Anne Whiting

present

***

"You're late."

He smiled. That's a good sign.

"Sorry, won't happen again. Darn Bugs."

"I used to have one."

"You like the word *used*."

Frown. Damn. I didn't want to make him frown. Say something, say something NICE! Quick! He's going in back and you won't see him for hours!

"By the way," Anne called; Gene turned and looked at her, "thanks for

last night."

"Last night?"

"Yeah. . ."

Oh SHIT. It really DIDN'T mean anything. Oh God! Now what, back pedal, back pedal!

"Uh. . . it was. . . umm. . . nice."

He scrunched his face. He looked younger to her then.

"Okay, then. Better get to work."

"Okay, then."

More billing. Yuck. I can't stand this job. At least I know what I DON'T want to do with my life. So what DO I want to do? Hard part. God he's cute. I wonder how old he is. He's got to be at least 30. He's pretty young to own a business. I wonder if he has a lot of money. I wonder what he looks like naked. I bet he kisses good. I hate guys who slobber all over me and the way he held my face I bet he kisses so tender, so clean. I bet he'd go real slow. . . God I've wanted a guy to...RRRRRRRRRIIIIIIIIIIIIIIIIIIINNNNNNNNNNNNNNNNNGGGG G

"Whiting's Tannery."

***

"So what you're telling us is that he has multiple sclerosis."

"You can see for yourself. Here are the sclerotic lesions."

Oh my God. I remember a lady who had MS—she got shots. . .in her eye! She was all fucked up! She always creeped me out with that eye. Oh SHIT!

"Is it curable?"

"No but it's manageable. Many people your age, Eugene," Dr. Pepori

stared matter-of-factly at Gene, "lead successful lives. I suggest we

begin treatment right away. Here's a prescription for IF injections."

NO NO NONONNNNOOOOO SHOTS!!!!!!

Doctors are like comedians, they know when they're losing

their audience.

"Here," Dr. Pepori said, pushing a stack of pamphlets into Anne's

hands, "the best thing you can do is educate yourself and, Eugene,

make sure you stop at the front desk on your way out to re-schedule."

The doctor elevated Gene's charge sheet with sausage-fingers while Anne watched the paper like a hawk to a mouse until inside the car when Gene set the sheet down. . .

GRAB IT!!!!   *$600!!!! You've got to be FUCKIN' kidding!*

. . . to put on his seatbelt. "Now why did you do that?"

"I wanted to see how much that prick charged us for 10 minutes of his time."

Gene smiled, "Well you know it took at least 5 minutes for him to look at my MRI."

Anne laughed. He always made her laugh.

***

"Come on, kid, you can do it!"

"AARRGGGHHH"

"Push it, dammit! You can DO IT! PUSH!"

"AAHHH"

"Decent. Have you gone up?"

"Since when?"

"Smart ass."

"That's why you love me, Bill."

"Keep talkin' and you'll remind me the 100 reasons I oughta kick your fanny to the curb."

"Thanks for the spot. You know," Anne put on her best flirt-eyes, "you're the best!"

"Flatterer."

"Honest Abe!"

"Who said Abe was honest? Never trust a politician kid."

"Can I get another spot?"

"Ya gonna' whimp out on me," he grinned, "like last set?"

"No SIR!"

"Awright. You called it now you gotta get it."   ***

"I think we should get a second opinion."

"Me too."

"Any ideas?"

"I know a guy who has MS. He's real fit: runner/skier (I think) he goes to a clinic just for MS."

"Where is it?"

"Details—I'll get them."

Anne drove. Gene's left arm had been bothering him. So had his left leg. Ever since they'd met he'd had a limp but he'd started holding his arm like it hung—slung. Anne said he needed to go the doctor.

Gene protested, "You send me to the doctor for every little thing! Remember?"

Giving head she felt a bump in Gene's scrotum and fun stopped. Doctor's appointment that afternoon. It turned out: a vessel engorged with blood; Gene and the doc had a good laugh at that.

Anne knew. That sneaking-sinking would—one day— capsized waves carrying him away. . .

The arm turned out to be a problem. X-ray said, "bones good."

Basic neurological test said, "something wrong. send to

$600-neurologist."

Then Anne decided, "educate selves!"

***

"I'm sorry," the university librarian said, "but you can't check out

books unless you're a student or purchase a library card."

"I JUST graduated two months ago."

"I know but if you're not currently enrolled you can't check out

books."

Anne sucked in her breath. Her view:

University=bureaucraticBS. Of course it didn't help she'd changed

her major ten times in the course of 5 years in earning a PE degree.

"How much is a library card?"

"$50.00"

"What!"

"I know. But it's good for a year and it helps support the library!

Plus, you get a nice newsletter."

*I can't FUCKING believe this SHIT! I JUST graduated. What kind of
fucking country is this that information COSTS! Doctors. Libraries.
It's a FUCKIN' conspiracy!*

"It's all I have," Anne said, handing the woman two twenties, one five,

two ones and three dollars in quarters.

"It's due back in one week."

"Hold on. One week? When I was a student it was three."

"It's different for community members than it is for students."

Anne grabbed the book, "Multiple Sclerosis: What Everyone Needs to

Know," and stormed out the door.

So that's it, eh? This is 'WELCOME to the FUCKIN' real world'.
Great.

A parking ticket tucked up her windshield.

FUCK

She threw it on the passenger seat.

I'm not fucking paying it. They can find me, since "I'm JUST A
COMMUNITY member!

***

"Will you marry me?"

I can't believe it. I never thought anyone... and it's here. In this place. I hate the smell of this place. ANSWER him dummy!

"Yes. You didn't have to ask."

His lips taste so good. I knew it before I ever kissed them that they would and his arms, just like they are right now, my God, I wish I was Midas and we'd both turn to gold statues this way. Wait! Okay. That's right. Everyone's gone. Oh yeah!

***

"It is my professional opinion that your symptoms are NOT from multiple sclerosis."

Anne hadn't learned of untamed tongues: "But what about the lesions on the MRI?"

AND what about all the FUCKING research I've done on MS for the last 6 months we've been waiting to see YOU Dr. JACKASS!

"There are lesions on your MRI," he said, looking at Gene. Never at Anne, "but it is unclear as to whether or not they are newly formed lesions or if they've been there, say, your whole life."

Anne went at him again, "So you're saying that these lesions could have ALWAYS been there?"

Getting brushed off by egotistical men meant getting her back into it.

"Yes, could have."

"What COULD have caused them?"

Again, looking only at Gene, "Any number of things."

Anne: "Such as?"

"High fever, viral infection, certain toxins, a great many things can cause lesions in the brain but the point is that you, EUGENE, have Parkinson's disease."

For once, Anne was quiet—inside and out.

***

"I'm sorry Anne, your card is expired."

"Oh come on, Shirley. Can't you cut me some slack?"

"Sorry kiddo."

Anne liked it when Shirley called her kiddo. It reminded her of Bill.

It reminded her that once, in what seemed the story of someone else's

life, she was young enough to be called such. . .

I wonder how Bill is?

"That will be $65.00."

"You went up?"

"Yeah, you should see my property taxes! You want ALL of these

books?"

"Yes please."

"Got a box?"

"Sure do. I come prepared but it's not a box. They don't hold up as

well. I've found that laundry baskets do the job best with 20 books

and over."

"I think you're the only student to check out so many books."

"Correction—former student."

"Ah, yes. Hey look, this one, 'Neurotransmitters Volume 16: Dopamine,' has never been checked out before."

"I bet if you look close, most of these babies are losing their virginity today!"

"Oh stop! You're making me blush."

"Hey, Shirley, you married?"

"Why, you gay?"

"I can't believe you'd ask me that. NO! But I used to know this guy you'd be perfect for."

"Sorry kiddo. Married, going on 25 this year."

"Wow! Congratulations!"

"What's wrong?"

"Oh . . . nothing. I just, uh, remembered I have to . . . go."

***

"Manganese-Induced Parkinsonism" J of Neuro, June 9, 2003"

Okay. This looks promising. Manganese is a metal. Chromium is a metal. He's been exposed to hexavalent chromium from the time he was born until now at the tannery. I think I remember some other thing, a movie, boobs, hold on . . . it's coming. . . my darn brain doesn't work like I want it to sometimes. . . some scandal. I'll Google chromium movie. AH, there it is. Mental note: rent movie. Okay back to the journal article. Please let this one have full text, PLEASE. . . SHIT! Abstract only. DAMN this FUCKING SHIT! This is an outrage! Information should not cost $30 a pop. I can't afford this damn education.

***

"Genevieve!"

"She'll be here soon baby."

"Don't lie. She won't come! She'll never come! She'll never forgive me."

"It wasn't your fault."

"I told her to leave."

"Her mother, not her."

"I should have stopped her."

"Which her?"

"Genevieve. . . Genevieve. . . my darling little Genevieve."

"I'm so sorry Gene."

"I know . . . I know. . . don't cry. . . don't. . . I need you to be strong."

I've always had to be strong.

"I can't help it. I'm sorry. I never used to be so weak."

"You're not weak because you cry but because you lie."

***

"Hey Anne," Kim called out from behind the desk.

Anne walked up, smile on her face. Everyone noticed Anne's smiles.
They swear she'd been smiling since the day she was born because no
one ever saw her any other way.

"Yeah, Kim."

"I got you something."

"Aw shucks," Anne poked Kim's arm, "it's not my birthday."

"I KNOW. I took your application, remember."

"You're not trying to hit on me are you?"

"I can't believe you'd say something like that! You know I'm happily
married."

"I sure do. And you got one of the finest guys in this shitty city."

"Do I see a frown-smile-upside down? I could set you up with a
REAL nice guy in a heartbeat!"

"Not on your life! Hey, I gotta' get on the road so we'd better get this
hurried up okay?"

    Kim handed Anne a book.

"I know you like to read."

"Says who?"

"I see books in your backseat all the time."

"I hate riding trains."

"I can't afford a car."

"Sucks to be you!"

"That's not nice and after I got you a present and everything."

"Now don't go cryin'"

"Don't worry about lil' ol' me. I may be small but I'm STRONG!"

Kim imitated Anne and flexed her biceps.

Anne read the title, "Schott's Original Miscellany."

She held it so Kim could read the title at the same time, "And you

thought of me be…cause…of…why???"

"I don't know."

"I luv ya' Kim but I gotta' go. See ya!"

***

He's on fire again. Every night the same burning. Flaming from the inside out but shivering, not really shivering but convulsing. His pillow's drenched with sweat and saliva. It smells. I don't care I love him. I shouldn't kiss his neck like that, it seems to make him twitch harder. His toe is arching up again, oh God, help him please, the tremors are coming. He's tensing! God help him. Help me. Help me find an answer.

***

"Oh my God. Oh my God."

"You like that don't you."

"You know I do."

"That?"

"Oh yes. DEFINITELY that! that! THAT!!!"

"Are you okay?"

"Yeahh… just a little out of breath."

"Was it okay?"

"You don't even have to ask me that because you know DARN well how much pleasure you give me. Can I return the favor?"

"You don't even have to ask."

"I love you. I love you so very much Gene."

"Don't cry."

"I can't help it. See what a blubbering baby you've turned me into."

"It's the multiples' fault."

"Can I make you cry?"

"You have before."

. . .and after. . .

"Ashes to ashes. . ."

"I'm so sorry."

"I'm sorry for your loss."

"Is there anything I can do?"

"Call me if you need anything."

"Remember, I'm here for you."

"I can't believe he's dead. He was a good man."

*He was a good man goodgoodgoood man goodman mangood hehehe
heehaw hehaw*
ha ha hahaaa   I will not let you die in vain!

***

"There is something I haven't told you."

Her head was hurting. She'd had headaches for years. Ever since she could remember. Though it seemed she'd forgotten everything before Gene.

"What is it?"

"Bad."

He's leaving me for another woman

"I'm broke."

"What do you mean?"

"The business is nearly bankrupt. I've borrowed as much as I can. Almost all of the accounts have been turned over to collections and I don't know what to do. I'm so sorry."

He loves me

She pulled his head to her chest, smelling the woody smell of cedar in his hair.

"Don't worry, baby. We'll figure it out."

"I feel like I've let you down."

"With money, I'd have to have been up to be let down and I've been poor my whole life—except I'm rich knowing you."

She kissed him soft and slow. "The world can go Fuck All. All I need is you."

"There is one other thing."

Oh now don't you dare tell me it's another woman!

"If I die you'll be set."

"Set?"

"I figure after paying all the debts I've made you'll have enough, if you're wiser than I've been, to live the rest of your life very comfortably."

"I don't want to talk about you dying."

"You know I'm dying."

She turned her back to him. He snuggled into her crying-curve.

"I'm going to a better place."

"You are my better place."

He turned her face to his, "Jesus loves me. He loves you too."

"Then why is he doing this?"

"He will work the ugliest, cruelest, most nefarious act into a miracle for our good. . . if we're faithful to Him."

I wish I could. . .

"I want to believe. . . I really do."

He hugged her tightly, swaying her slightly—side-to-side—like a mother-child.

"That's the first step, my beautiful wife. That's the first step."

***

"You want to rent how many storage units?"

"Twenty."

"Twenty 10x24s?"

"Yes."

"Drugs?"

"Absolutely not."

"Then what?"

"Water."

"Water?"

"Yeah. I'm paranoid about drinking water. I want to stockpile bottled

water in case Hell breaks loose."

"You're in D.C.—too late!" He laughed and pushed the

app—attached to its plastic clipped board—at her. "It'll cost you."

"I'll pay the year—today."

***

"Hello, is this Whiting's Tannery?"

"Whom may I say is calling?"

"Naturo Chemicals."

"Yes, this is Whiting's Tannery."

"We have a question regarding your order."

"Yes."

"We just want to verify that you want to double your sodium dichromate."

"That's correct. We're expanding business."

"Excellent. We'll ship it out this afternoon."

"Thank you."

RRRRRRRRRIIIIIIIIIIIIIIIIIIIIIINNNNNNNNNNNNNGGGGGGGGG

"Hello."

"Is this Whiting's Tannery?"

"May I ask who is calling?"

"Safford's Leathery."

"I'm sorry. Whiting's Tannery is no longer in business might I suggest . . ."   ***

Dear Diary

I put him in the ground today. I'm home. Our home. Echoes
canyon-deadness. God. Even the wallpaper is missing him. But. . .
he finally saw. . . finally knew I could tell the truth. . . Vieve came and
took him away—all these fucking accidents. Mothers killing
daughters with cars. Metals killing men with barbs in their brains…

he said I should be happy when he died because his suffering'd end.
So would Christ's—being reunited with his child that he suffered
for—so long ago—hanging on that cross while his Father poured out
Wrath for everything wrong Gene had ever done. . .

but I wasn't raised like him. My parents died when I was too young to
even remember them. I grew up with cousins who beat me, raped me,
kicked me to the street when I was barely a teenager. Everything I've
gotten in this world I've gotten by fighting because I've
LIVED DOG,   still. . .

he wanted me. . . I want. . . to believe but something is wrong in me.
I'm filled redness & volcano-magma & I'm bursting, molten—
/rock\/mineral\. . ./ metal\

***

"You're right on time."

"Aren't I always?"

"Yes Ma'am."

"You're the only one who's ever called me ma'am."

"Sorry Ma'am."

"I suppose I'm that much older than you."

"No. Just beautiful and commanding."

"Commanding? Of what?"

"Appreciation."

Anne smiled. It was the first real one since Gene had died.

"You're quite the flatterer. Didn't Kim tell you. I'm a dyke."

The guard smiled.

"If you're a dyke then so am I."

"Oh yeah, Jamie, I didn't know you like dressing up like a woman."

"I don't."

He buzzed her through and watched her as she dollied the days' water to the elevators [|] after she'd unloaded and was about to walk out the door Jamie called out, "Can I buy you a coffee sometime."

"I don't drink."

"Coffee?"

"Water," she said, pointing to the side of her truck's logo.

***

"What's wrong baby?"

"Nothing, nothing."

I must have done something wrong. He's lost his erection again. I miss him. Do something. Don't let him know. Do something.

"Lie back. That's it. Let me do the work. . . God. . . you taste so good. That's it. Oh my God, that's it baby. . ."

"I'm coming."

He came. He was soft in my mouth and came. That was the most BEAUTIFUL THING I've ever known!
"Did that feel okay?"

"Yes, yes, yes. It felt wonderful. Thank you."

"Uh, did you orgasm. . . I mean I know you came but did you climax?"

"Yes I did."

"How was it?"

"Intense, why?"

"Because you weren't hard."

"I know. Was it bad for you?"

"No! It was fucking awesome!"

"Well. I haven't heard you use that explicative for a while."

"Sorry, it just slipped out."

Anne snuggled up to Gene's chest. He stroked her back and shoulders and then started ||| sleep.

It's beginning again.

She watched his mouth gape. She waited.

There. . . there. . . it's happening. . .

He couldn't breathe. His lungs shook his body until he sucked hard air. His legs shook.

It's coming. . .

His hand wrested her shoulder. His fingergrips viced hard and deep. . .

It's hurting and only halfway to where he'll shift. It'll leave a mark.

One final shudder. He opened his eyes, released his grasp, and—with dreamy blue eyes—smiled, "I love you Anne."

"I love you Gene. Can I snuggle your back?"

"Sure."

Drifting back to sleep he whispered, "There is a verse in the Bible which has been translated into more than 1100 languages. Would you like to know what it is?"

"Sure," Anne replied, closing her eyes and pressing her nose into the crack of his back's spine.

"FOR GOD SO LOVED THE WORLD,

THAT HE GAVE HIS ONLY BEGOTTEN SON,

THAT WHOSOEVER BELIEVETH IN HIM SHOULD NOT PERISH,

BUT HAVE EVERLASTING LIFE."

Anne opened her eyes.

***

"Kim, I need an appointment with BossMan."

She giggled. "Nothing too serious I hope."

"I'm quitting."

Kim's eyes got big, her cheeks and nose-tip turned scarlet.

"Ummm. . . he has an opening at. . .uh. . . 10:00am."

"That'll do."

Anne turned to walk out but Kim ran in front of her.

"You mean that's it! Five years and that's it! I thought we were friends."

Kim put her face in her hands. She'd always been simple. She loved or hated. There was no middle ground.

"It's nothing personal."

"It was personal to me!"

Kim returned to her desk.

***

Dear Diary,

It's been a long time, my dear old friend. So much since…Gene died.
I've found someone who might work. It will take some time, more for
me than for him. I can't bear another's hands, another's eyes—it
makes me sick that he even 'love' and I know he does. I must
overcome this aversion—for Gene, for Gene, for Gene—My Beloved
how I miss you!

***

"The units are empty I'm checking out."

"So where you going to store all that water now?"

"There's no water to store."

"WHAT?"

"That's right." Anne patted her tummy, "It's ALL GONE."

"Now I've seen it all."

The manager signed the contract then looked up at Anne.

"Hey wait a minute, you mean you're okay with drinking regular water now?"

"No. I'm moving."

"Damn. Five years and you've been my best customer."

"Oh yeah. Why?"

"You paid cash."

***

"Put the load in the back."

The driver nodded. After the hexavalent chromium was unloaded and he was having Anne sign off the receipt he looked around,

"The place looks empty."

"It is."

"So why you need all this crap," he said pointing to the crates.

"This place is our storage unit now. We built a new facility on the other side of town."

"Oh. Business must be good."

"Yeah. It's good."

"Maybe I should'a became a tanner instead of a trucker."

Anne smiled at him. He was big and strong. He reminded her of Bill and the gang at the gym.

* * *

"So this is what I do when I really need help. I pray for the Holy Spirit

to guide me in the Living Word of the Bible."

"Living?"

"Yes."

"It's ink. . .on paper. . ."

"It's Living."

"Does it breed, breathe, shit?"

"You'll see, someday. . . I hope. It's truly magnificent when it

happens, when God gives you that gift."

*To be delusional? But he's not. I KNOW him. He's the most sane
and smart person I've EVER known. Why does he believe all this? I'd
be totally freaked out if it didn't seem to bring him so much happiness.
. . and peace.*
"Like now. I see you're doubting."

"Me? A skeptic, nahhh. Never!"

He grinned. "Lord, I pray the Holy Spirit will guide me in Your

Living Word to give Anne just what You know she needs to hear this

very moment. I ask this in Jesus' name. Amen." He opened the book

and began:

*To every thing there is a season, and a time to every purpose under the
heaven:
A time to be born, and a time to die;
A time to plant, and a time to pluck up that which is planted;*

A time to kill, and a time to heal;
A time to break down, and a time to build up;
A time to weep, and a time to laugh;
A time to mourn, and a time to dance;
A time to cast away stones, and a time to gather stones together;
A time to embrace; and a time to refrain from embracing;
A time to get, and a time to lose;
A time to keep, and a time to cast away;
A time to rend; and a time to sew;
A time to keep silence, and a time to speak;
A time to love, and a time to hate;
A time of war, and a time of peace. . . Ecclesiastes

"Anne, I need you to listen to this next bit carefully, okay?"

"I've been listening."

"I mean really listen, with that part of you that wants to know Christ."

Anne nodded.

What profit hath he that worketh in that wherein he laboureth?

I have seen the travail,
which God hath given to the sons of men to be exercises in it.

> He hath made every thing beautiful in his time:
> also he hath set the world in their heart,
so that no man can find out the work that God maketh from the beginning
to the end. . .

I said in mine heart,
God shall judge the righteous and the wicked:
for there is a time there for every purpose and for every work.

Gene took Anne's hands and put them onto the open pages of

the Bible.

"Want to try?"

"Try what?"

"Praying for guidance."

"You do it for me. You're the one who's already good at this."

He smiled, "It's a start, at least. Lord I ask that you send your Holy Spirit to be with Anne. You know her heart, her spirit, her soul. You created her, knit her in Your own hands and she is your child. Please guide her in Your will, Lord. In Jesus' name I ask this and I ask You, Lord, to just let Anne know You. Let her feel Your presence, Your touch, as You have blessed me to feel. Amen."

Anne turned the pages. She shut the book. Then opened it. She didn't feel like reading. She didn't see anything but she didn't want to disappoint Gene. She knew he wanted her to see something.

God please let me see SOMETHING! It means so much to him and he believes in you. Doesn't that count for SOMETHING?"

then **LETTERS** jumped BLACKSTRONG from the rest and Anne read aloud:

Think not that I am come to send peace on earth:
I came not to send peace, but a sword.

For I am come to set a man at variance against his father,
  And the daughter against her mother,

And the daughter-in-law against her mother-in-law.
And a man's foes shall be they of his own household.

He that loveth father or mother more than me is not worthy of me:
And he that loveth son or daughter more than me is not worthy of me.
And he that taketh not his cross, and followeth after me, is not worthy of me.
He that findeth his life shall lose it:
And he that loseth his life for my sake shall find it.
                                        Mathew

Anne looked up. Gene was crying. She started to cry too but she knew she was crying for the wrong reason.

***

"What are you doing?"

"Inventory."

"Of what?"

Gene watched Anne scratching, feverishly, onto a yellow legal pad.

"Chemicals."

"What for?"

"Oh, nothin' I was thinkin' of sellin' them @ auction or the black market," she smiled.

"Hmmm. Is the billing caught up?"

"Yeah. I wish the collections would get caught up—somewhere else."

"Me too."

Anne had gone for a laugh. Lately, Gene hadn't been laughing much. It seemed it was getting harder and harder for him to get around the shop.

Even Dan, the mechanic, noticed; "Hey, Annie, what's wrong with Gene? Hit that 5-year itch?"

"What 5-year itch?"

"They say every 5 years a man gets itchy, you know, down there,"

pointing to his crotch.

Anne smirked, "Well in your case Dan, I hear they got ointments for

those kinds of things now-a-days," and went back to writing on her

pad:

> **Ammonia,**
> **Chrometan,**
> **Chrome tan. . .**

***

"So you want'a get a coffee after work?"

"You talkin' to me?"

"Okay. That was cheesy."

Jamie laughed. "Why the change of heart? I've been askin' you for months."

"Cause you've been asking me for months."

"You like Starbucks?"

"Got any coffee at your place?"

Jamie's eyes got big. His eyebrows raised, his right a little higher than his left—Anne noticed.

"Uh. . .yeah."

***

Black Binder #1:

Q&As

Q: What is Parkinson's disease?

A: They don't know WHAT it is. They know what happens. The

cells that make Gene move are dying and they can't stop it.

Matter-of-fact, the medicines they keep feeding him like candy

actually kill whatever "dopamine" cells that are left standing from

whatever it is that's killin' them in the first place.

NOTE: What's dopamine? What is this Toxin-Induced Parkinsonism

I've read about? What toxins has Gene been exposed to? Maybe it

has something to do with the leather tanning...

***

"Hi, Dan. Mind if I come in?"

"Suit yourself."

"May I sit?"

"Seems you can do whatever you damn-well please!"

"You're angry with me. . . I can understand that. . . "

"You're all of what, 25 years old? I've spent more years at Whiting's than you've been alive so don't come in here, to MY home, and tell me you understand. You don't understand SHIT! Now get out. . . if you PLEASE!"

Anne walked to the door but before she left she turned to watch Dan sitting in his recliner. She saw the shaking arm and leg—the face hanging like a painting though he was mad as hell. She knew without asking that either he'd already been diagnosed—or soon would be— with Parkinson's disease.

later past (7 months after Anne's visit)

Obituaries:
Dan Martin died Friday evening at Metro Hospital from complications associated with Parkinson's disease. He served in the Korean Conflict as a Marine. Per his request there will be no funeral service. He is survived by his nephew, Lt. Karl Martin, USMC.

***

TEXTBOOK: <u>MANGANESE</u>

MANGANESE IS A HARD, GRAY-WHITE METAL THAT HAS MANY PROPERTIES SIMILAR TO THOSE OF IRON, ITS NEIGHBOR ON THE PERIODIC TABLE. IT NOT ONLY LOOKS LIKE IRON, BUT LIKE IRON IT CORRODES IN MOIST AIR.

Note: it removes hydrogen gas on batteries so they keep functioning (the electrical charge would fail to transmit if the excess hydrogen [a by-product from the chemicals used to create electrical charge in the battery] from the electrode weren't removed).

Manganese poisoning can cause parkinsonism. Manganese is a metal. Maybe other metals can cause parkinsonism. . . I remember something. . . some metal we used. . . SHIT what was it???. . .Kro... no...wheels. . . I HATE the way my brain works. Wheels, what the hell do wheels have to do with anything??? Grills? Grills, Kro...chrome. CHROME! That's it! Chromium.

***

"You got a nice place here."

"Thanks. How do you like it?"

"I said it was nice, what more do you want?"

"I mean your coffee?"

"Oh, black."

"Me too."

"The coincidences never stop," Anne mumbled as she looked over the pictures on the bookshelf.

She always thought it was odd that people put pictures where books were supposed to be but this time she was glad. She wanted to know everything she could; about James R. Pickett pictures were the quickest answers.

***

"Where on earth did you learn to do THAT?"

"Right here."

"Where, your bed?"

"No. With you."

Anne stared at him, then punched him in the shoulder.

"Get out'a here!"

"It's true."

"So you're telling me you've NEVER done that before?"

"That's what I'm tellin' yuse," Gene pushed his tongue to the side of his cheek.

"Give it up! You do the WORST Brando I've EVER seen."

Anne settled her ear just over his heart.

Ka-thudda, ka-thudda, ka-thudda

"You've really never done that to anyone else before?"

"I promise. . . has anyone ever done that to you before?"

She squeezed him so tight that the "Chhh, chhhh, chhh" of her ear mixed with Gene's heart beating.

"No. No one's ever done THAT before."

Gene pushed Anne back so he could look her in the eye.

"What 'that' are we talking about?"

Anne rolled away, tucking her knees to her chest. Gene snuggled up behind her.

"It's okay, Anne. You don't have to tell me."

"I want to. . . I really do. . . it's just hard for me."

"I know."

"You do?"

"Yes. That's why I'm so happy. You finally let someone in, past the walls, and see. . . the world didn't come to an end—did it?"

She rolled to face him. Tears. Snotty nose.

"No. And you know what?"

"What," Gene asked.

"That felt FUCKING AWESOME!"

***

"Hi Steve."

"Hi Anne."

"Can I come in."

"You bet. How's Gene doing?"

"Not so good, but thanks for asking."

"Can I get you something to drink?"

"No thanks."

There was an awkward silence.

"Well, what brings you round my way?"

"I just wanted to see how everyone was doing now that the shop was closed."

"Oh I can't complain."

"We're really sorry we had to close up."

"Yeah, me too. I was only 5 years from retirement."

"I know. But with all the other tanneries moving overseas ours just wasn't making the money it would have needed to give you guys what we would have liked to. You know, Steve, if we could have we would have given you a really nice early-retirement."

"I know, Anne. Gene and his family are gold."

"So you knew Gene's dad too?"

"Knew the whole bunch."

"Can I ask you something?"

"Sure…don't know as I'll have an answer though."

"Do you remember if Gene's dad's hands ever shook?"

Steve rubbed his temple for a few minutes.

"Now that you mention it, I remember one time he asked me to go and get some chemicals from the paint store. " Steve looked up laughing.

"What's so funny?" Anne asked.

"Well I couldn't imagine what he would have wanted from a paint store and he said I wasn't smart enough to know it even if he told me. Anyhow, he wrote out the name of it on a piece of paper."

Anne's heart began to race. "Do you remember what the chemical was?"

"Oh Goodness sakes, no!" He laughed harder. "I just remember that when he wrote it down his hand was shaking something fierce."

Anne stood to go.

"Thank you, Steve. You've helped me out more than you know."

Steve stood and began to walk to the door. At first, it was like he was frozen and then it was like a blast of heat melted the ice and he started stepping so fast he almost tripped by the time he reached for

Anne's arm.

"Don't be a stranger," he called out to her as she walked to her

Volkswagon.

passed away (1 year after Anne's visit)

Obituaries:
Steven R. Fliegal died Thursday morning at Sister Mercy's Hospital
from complications associated with Parkinson's disease. He is
survived by his wife, Caroline and his son, Nathaniel. The funeral
service is scheduled for Sunday at Rolling Acres Memorial Park.

***

"Happy birthday to you…happy birthday to you…haaaapppppeeeee birthday my dear luuuuuvvvver. Happy Birthday to you! And many more!!"

"What did you get me?"

"That's what I love about you, Gene."

"What?"

"You're just a big kid! Close your eyes. Okay. . . ready?"

"Couldn't be more ready if I tried. . .   OOOMMMPHH! What the heck?"

He opened his eyes to one of the largest binders he'd ever seen. It wasn't that it was too long or too tall but that it was too thick.

"What's this?"

"All the research I've done in the last three months."

He opened the cover to a photocopy,

Chromium.
1960, first laser (ruby laser/ruby crystal of Al2O3 with small chromium contamination) by Theodore H. Maiman. Under certain circumstances chromium is radioactive. Text noted, "Chromium compounds should be handled with care because many of them are toxic."

"So what do you think?"

"Uh. . . I don't really know what to say."

"Well. . . are you going to read it?"

He looked at the binder. He lifted it up and down. "This thing must weigh ten pounds."

"Oh at least. You wouldn't believe how many reams of paper I've gone through."

He smiled. "I believe it."

He continued reading:

Chromium
It is the 10th most abundant metal in the Earth's crust.
Uses: leather tanning, anti-corrosive, film processing, chromatic aspect of audio, metal products, computer/electrical.
Synonym for Chromium: Chrome
Synonym for Chromium [hexavalent]: Chromium [VI] compounds.
                    [trivalent]: Chromium [III] the (as we know of) non-toxic form in vitamins and shit.
Synonyms for Cobalt-chromium-molybdenum alloy:
Akrit, AMS, F 75, HS 21, Protasul-2, Vinertia, Vitallium, Zimalloy, AF22, AF22-130, AISI 318L, Alloy 2205, Arosta 4462, AST, Avesta 2205, Avesta 223FAL, CR22, DIN 1.4462, ES 2205, FAL 223,
Iron alloy,
Mann AF-22,
Nirosta 4462, NKK-Cr22, Novonox FALC 223, NU 744 LN, NU stainless 744 LN, Remanit 4462, SAF 2205,
Sandvik SAF 2205,
SS 2377,
Stainless Steel 2205, Uddeholm Nu 744 LN, UHB 744LN, UNS S31803,
Uranus 45N,
UR45N, Vallourec VS22, VEW A903, VLX 562, VS 22,
X2CrNiMoN2253
Z2CND22.5AZ, 744LN
Synonyms for Ferrochrome:

Carbon ferrochromium, Chrome ferroalloy, Chromium alloy [base], [Cr, C, Fe, N, Si], Chromium ferroalloy, Ferrochrome, Ferrochromium

Synonyms for Iron-nickel-chromium alloy:
AFNOR ZfeNC45-36, AISI 332, Alloy 880, Alloy 800NG, DIN 1.4876, IN 800, Incology 800,
Iron alloy [base], [Fe 39-47, Ni 30-35, Cr 19-23, Mn 0-1.5, Si 0-1, Cu 0-0.8, Al 0-0.6, Ti 0-0.6, C 0-0.1],
JIS NCF 800, N 800, NCF 800, NCF 800 HTB, NCF steel,
Nickel 800,
Nicrofer 3220,
POLDI AKR 17, Pyromet 800, Sanicro 31, Thermax 4876, TIG N800

Synonyms for Nickel-chromium alloy:
Chromel C, Kh15N60N,
Nichrome,
Nickel alloy [base][Ni 57-62, Fe 22-28, Cr 14-18, Si 0.8-1.6, Mn 0-1, C 0-0.2],
PHKh, Tophet C

Synonyms for Basic Chromic Sulfate
Basic chromium sulfate, Chromedol,
Chrometan,
Chrome tan,
Chromium hydroxide sulfate [Cr(OH))SO4)], Chromium sulfate, Monobasic chromium sulfate,
Peachrome,
Sulfuric acid/chromium salt/basic,
Neochromium

Synonyms for Chromic acetate:
Acetic acid/chromium [3+]salt
Chromium acetate, Chromium[III]acetate, Chromium triacetate

Synonyms for Chromic chloride:
Chromium chloride [CrCl3], Chromium[III] chloride, Chromium trichloride, Trichorochromium

Synonyms for Chromic hydroxide:
Chromic acid [H3CrO3]
Chromium hydroxide [CrOH)3]
Chromium[III] hydroxide,
Chromium (3+) hydroxide
Chromium trihydroxide

Synonyms for Chromic nitrate:
Chromium nitrate, Chromium(3+) nitrate, Chromium [III] nitrate, Chromium trinitrate,

Nitric acid, Chromium (3+) Salt!!!!

While he read, Anne whispered,

"The only things I know that have so many names for the same things are the accounts accountants personally account for and the laws lawyers debate to finagle greatest return."

Gene laughed.

Anne read over his shoulder. . .and thought:

*My head is killing me!!! This shit is worse than Kinesiology in PE.
How in the hell am I going to make sense out of all this? Lord, if
you're listening...I could really use a break right about now. My head
feels like it's going to burst. That reminds me of Gene's Chinese
model. Bursting. I wonder what that felt like. I know he said it was
uncomfortable but I can't imagine what it would be like to have a cock
so big (or a pussy so small—or both :) that just to get in took half-
hour. My brain is that cunt—these scientific terms are the biggest
cock I've ever known! Like freakin' dildo from HELL. Oops, sorry
God, okay, back on track. God, I know I'm the worst person on the
Earth and I don't deserve a break. If anything I deserve to be sent
straight to hell but Gene is good. He loves you with all his heart.
Please help me, so I can find a way to help him...okay?*

Synonyms for Ferrochrome:
**Carbon ferrochromium, Chrome ferroalloy, Chromium alloy [base], [Cr, C, Fe,
N, Si], Chromium ferroalloy, Ferrochrome, Ferrochromium**
Synonyms for Iron-nickel-chromium alloy:
AFNOR ZfeNC45-36, AISI 332, Alloy 880, Alloy 800NG, DIN 1.4876, IN 800,
Incology 800,
Iron alloy [base], [Fe 39-47, Ni 30-35, Cr 19-23, Mn 0-1.5, Si 0-1, Cu 0-0.8, Al 0-
0.6, Ti 0-0.6, C 0-0.1],
JIS NCF 800, N 800, NCF 800, NCF 800 HTB, NCF steel,
Nickel 800,
Nicrofer 3220,
POLDI AKR 17, Pyromet 800, Sanicro 31, Thermax 4876, TIG N800

Synonyms for Nickel-chromium alloy:

Chromel C, Kh15N60N,
Nichrome,
Nickel alloy [base][Ni 57-62, Fe 22-28, Cr 14-18, Si 0.8-1.6, Mn 0-1, C 0-0.2],
PHKh, Tophet C

Synonyms for Basic Chromic Sulfate
Basic chromium sulfate, Chromedol,
Chrometan,
Chrome tan,
Chromium hydroxide sulfate [Cr(OH))SO4)], Chromium sulfate, Monobasic
chromium sulfate,
Peachrome,
Sulfuric acid/chromium salt/basic,
Neochromium

Synonyms for Chromic acetate:
Acetic acid/chromium [3+]salt
Chromium acetate, Chromium[III]acetate, Chromium triacetate

Synonyms for Chromic chloride:
Chromium chloride [CrCl3], Chromium[III] chloride, Chromium trichloride,
Trichorochromium

Synonyms for Chromic hydroxide:
Chromic acid [H3CrO3]
Chromium hydroxide [CrOH)3]
Chromium[III] hydroxide,
Chromium (3+) hydroxide
Chromium trihydroxide

These are important.
I remember reading somewhere about the oxidative process in
Parkinson's disease.
For every chemical reaction in the body there must be a
corresponding enzyme...what was it for dopamine...
Tyrosine...tyrosine...tyrosine HYDROXYLASE?

Synonyms for Chromic nitrate:
Chromium nitrate, Chromium(3+) nitrate, Chromium [III] nitrate, Chromium
trinitrate,
Nitric acid, Chromium (3+) Salt!!!!

THAT'S IT! The NO (nitric oxide) scavenger studies for PD patients!
The oxidative stress and PD studies.
The excess iron theory for oxidative stress in PD.
The reduction of CrVI to CrIII inside the cell creating???? Nitric
Oxide/Acid?
The pH of CrVI and the excess H+ ions means the equation MUST
balance!
There must be Oxygen to yield H20.
The radioactive reaction in the 60's laser— CrIII in cells setting up
cross-firing-relay between the cells and stimulating too much
oxygen???But how?

How can the CrIII (which is non-toxic) keep producing toxic effect
within the cell?

Gene stopped reading and looked up at Anne, whose eyes were darting

back and forth across the opened pages.

"Honey," he said, "I don't understand."

"Well, I'm no expert," she replied, "but from how I see it so far it's

like this. . ."

***

"Ummm. Good coffee."

"Thanks."

"So who're all the pictures of?"

"What, you want a blow-by-blow?"

"Yeah, humor me."

He laughed, "That won't be hard. This here's my mom and dad. My best friend, Mikey. My brother, Brian. The rest are unimportant."

"The rest. . .meaning?"

"Just girls."

"Just girls? I see."

"Friends."

"A friend of mine once told me guys don't have girls for friends. They have friends that are girls so that they can get some during a 'friendly intervention' because girls always get themselves into some crisis."

"Well I don't know who your friend was, but I'm tellin' you these girls were just friends."

"Were?"

"Yeah."

An awkward silence.

"So where do your parents live," Anne piped.

"In the ground."

Damn! I haven't lost my touch, shit. Okay, say something. Recover. BE NICE!!!!

"I'm sorry for your loss."

"Thanks."

"What about your brother?"

"Same."

SHIT. That's it. I better get out of here before he kicks me out.

"I'm just saying all the wrong things. I'd better go."

"Don't. Please. It's better you know now anyhow."

"Know what?"

"I'm kind of a loner since Mom, Dad, and Brian got killed."

"Killed?"

"Yeah, drunk driver."

Anne put her hand on his shoulder. "I know what you mean."

"Yeah. . . about what?"

"About being a loner."

He nodded his head. "I figured that about you. That's why I wanted to get to know you better."

"That's so?"

"Sometimes people who've been through shit make the best companions."

"Why's that?"

"Neither notice how much the other stinks," he punched her in the arm, but Anne didn't smile.

It wasn't his words. It was her arm-nerves reflexively remembering Gene.

***

Anne took the birthday present from Gene's hands and threw it across the floor.

He cried out, "I'm sorry. I just don't understand what you're saying."

"It's because I'm fuckin' crazy!!!"

"You're not crazy. If anything you're brilliant! Please don't be angry with me because I don't understand. Let me try again."

"I CAN'T!"

"Why Not?"

"Because I don't understand it well-enough myself. How can I show you what I don't know yet?"

"Well," he said, calmness returning to his voice, "how about we just sit and talk. You don't have to SHOW me anything. You don't have to be an expert. I can see you've done a lot of work on my behalf. . ." He wrapped his arms around her shoulders and held her tight ". . . and I can't tell you how much that makes me feel loved."

***

How did that old saying go???? Lay 'em right the first time and you can walk all over 'em

"So what about your friend, Mikey?"

"He got killed in Iraq."

"Damn! I don't know about you, Jamie. I'm beginning to think you

might be a bad luck charm," Anne smiled and punched him back.

It hurt her to do it in the deepest part of her soul.

***

"Okay, you know about pH?"

"Yes. It deals with acidity and alkalinity."

"Right. It stands for 'potential hydrogen' and the values are found by using a negative logarithm of the hydrogen-ion concentration."

She grabbed a piece of paper and a pen:

$$(pH=log10^1 /[H+]$$

"Okay," Gene replied.

"This means that a pH of 1 is 10x more acidic than a pH of 2 AND the pH (potential hydrogen) of [milk of magnesia—magnesium hydroxide] is 10.5."

Gene sucked in a breath of air, "You're loosing me."

"Milk of Magnesia is from the metal magnesium."

"Okay."

"And magnesium (Mg) is a silvery white metal, class IIA element, that is chemically reactive."

"Okay, but this folder is all about chromium."

"I know. I know! Just be patient! I'm trying to get there. Oh FORGET IT!!! I'm too stupid for this!"

Gene pulled her back to him, "I'm doing the best I can," he said, "but I just don't get it. You're talking about magnesium but telling me that it's because of some type of chromium why I'm sick?"

"Yes...look at this letter."

He read the letter: Dear Anne,

Thank you for your kind letter. Heavy metals have been implicated in the pathogenesis of PD. Heavy metals especially lead and arsenic can produce membrane sodium-potassium ATPase inhibition and modulate intracellular calcium/magnesium ratios. They can act in the same way as digoxin (an endogenous membrane sodium-potassium ATPase inhibitor). They can add onto the action of digoxin. Thus lead and arsenic can activate the same membrane as sodium-potassium ATPase inhibition cascade. The treatment of such cases of toxic PD involves the use of membrane sodium-potassium ATPase stimulators like magnesium.

Chromium is a membrane sodium-potassium ATPase stimulator and is not toxic to the brain.

Yours sincerely,
Dr. Puruk

"So what this is saying is that chromium isn't toxic to the brain."

"No, what it's saying is that chromium stimulates sodium-potassium ATPase."

"And what does that mean? How does that relate to my Parkinson's disease?"

"I don't know. . .yet."   ***

Past past

Dear Dr. Berktrim,

    I have done research on a group occupationally exposed to hexavalent chromium. The results were drawn from employee records, personal testimonies, and physician's notes (where possible). I must tell you that nearly 50% of the people who lived past the age of 50 (for many died of cancer-related illness) developed some form of parkinsonism (or as otherwise noted: shaking palsy). These records/cases go back into the early 1920s for a leather tanning business. In total there are 150 people noted. I must tell you that I feel there is a relationship between people being exposed to toxic levels of hexavalent chromium and them, later, developing parkinsonism or Parkinson's disease.

Less past

Dear Ms. Whiting,

    First, I must tell you that there have been no studies showing any relation between chromium and parkinsonism that I am aware of. Second, what you describe is not reliable. There may have been records missing. There may have been people misdiagnosed and personal testimony and/or observation is the LEAST reliable form of research.

    I must tell you that your wording that hexavalent chromium exposure causes parkinsonism is very problematic. Definitive causative relationships are VERY difficult to prove.

    I can be of no further assistance to you except to suggest you might consider contacting an epidemiologist.

Dr. Berktrim

Arrogant son-of-a-bitch! What the hell is an epidemiologist?

Anne grabbed a dictionary.

EPIDEMIOLOGY—1. THE BRANCH OF MEDICINE DEALING WITH THE INCIDENCE AND PREVALENCE OF DISEASE IN LARGE POPULATIONS AND WITH DETECTION OF THE SOURCE AND CAUSE OF EPIDEMICS. 2. THE FACTORS CONTRIBUTING TO THE PRESENCE OR ABSENCE OF A DISEASE.

***

In a small apartment in Washington D.C. Anne woke. Naked.

Alone. Beside a note:

Annie,

I love you.

I've loved you since the first day I met you 5 years ago.

Will you marry me?

Jamie

Lay 'em right.

***

Dear Diary,

This will be my last entry into you. I am putting you into your own library. Someday, someone will come for you and you will be able to tell them who I am. How I've loved. When I lived—when I died. What I've done and why I've done it.

I am a terrorist. But according to the people who say hexavalent chromium can't do harm when ingested—(our own government)—I am NOT a terrorist because I have merely added to the water of every cooler in the United States Capitol Complex including: House Office Buildings, Senate Office Buildings, Library of Congress, U.S. Capitol, and U.S. Supreme Court a harmless chemical [when swallowed in water].

Concentrations of hexavalent chromium [100 times higher than the highest levels ever suffered by the people of the town of Hinckley, California] have been added for the last FIVE years. Why?

The Environmental Protection Agency promised to study ingested hexavalent chromium (sodium dichromate) for 1 month, 3 months, 6 months, 1 year, 2 years, and 5 years but NEVER published the findings past the 1 year study.   Now the United States politicians have all consumed hexavalent chromium. Their secretaries and their children who visit them at their office. The copy chasers. The mailroom. Everyone who's afraid to drink D.C.'s tap water—but has worked in this icon of Democracy—had better start reading what happened to those people from Hinckley.

And more than that—here is the scientific proof that hexavalent chromium can cause parkinsonism via . . .

&&&&&&&@@@@@@@&&&&&&&@@@@@@@^=+)~.

PART II's chapter O1

"Passports."

In Nelson—on the South Island of New Zealand—Anne and Jamie handed the official their passports.

"How long are you planning to stay in New Zealand?"

"Permanently."

"Visas please. Thank you."

"Financial disclosure. Thank you. Please go with this officer."

Jamie looked at Anne. He remembered the day he'd asked her to marry him.

"No," she said, "but I will never leave you and you will never be in need of anything as long as you're with me on ONE condition."

"What's that?"

"You tell me one thing you've always wanted to do."

"Live in New Zealand."

Later. . .

"This is a real nice house. It sits on an acre, great view of the ocean, small town, upscale neighborhood but no close neighbors. Pick of 'em as far as they go, I tell you."

"It'll be fine. Cash alright?"

The realtor's eyes got saucer-like, "Yeah, I think. I'll have to check with mi' boss. I don't know as I ever had someone buy a house with cash." She looked around, suddenly, "You don't keep that kinda' cash lyin' 'round I hope?"

Anne smiled, "Of course not. Royal Bank."

The lady eased, "Good, good. Very well then. Let's go to the office and we'll get all the paperwork done, eh?"

"Yes."

Anne put her arm through Jamie's, "So what do you think?"

"I think it's outrageously expensive and beautiful and more than I could have ever dreamed of."

He kissed her so tenderly that a moment—the world— disappeared. She—pear-aired hydrogen—suddenly crashed back into her—heavy-lead-self. . .*NOOOOO! Don't let him in!!!!*

Anne pulled away, "We'd better get the papers signed."

"Are you sure you can afford it?"

"When my husband died he left me very well provided for."

"You never told me you were married."

"You never asked the right question."

He grabbed her around her waist and kissed her neck. "Oh yeah, what other little secrets do you have that I should know about, eh?"

"Turning Kiwi already on me? Soon you'll be a beach bum surfing the days away."

"I don't like sharks."

"Me neither.

The realtor harumf'd.

In unison, Anne and Jamie laughed, then said, "Sorry."

After ALL expenses had been paid (Gene's business expenses: Anne's retribution) Anne was left with nearly half Gene's life insurance. She could have sold Gene's commercial property and recouped even more (for the land market in Gene's hometown had turned white-hot) but Anne had other plans for Whiting's Tannery.

Bank-draft noted=paid mortgage & the house belonged to Jamie and he burst, "How could you do this?"

"What?"

"I can't take this house? It's WAAYY too much! We're not even married! For Christ's sake, Anne, at least marry me!"

"Don't take Christ's name in vain."

Jamie raised his eyebrows—one higher than the other, "Since when did you get religion?"

"What makes you think I didn't have it?"

"Just a feeling I guess."

"Oh yeah, like THIS feeling. . ." Anne fell to her knees on the kitchen floor and pulled Jamie's shorts round his ankles.

It was the middle of winter, raining, but warm. It never would get too cool. It was a moist environment. Anne just knew God was providing for her—ever since Gene had died she'd felt a calling to do something important. Something that could have been squelched at every turn yet every turn seemed to keep her destiny right on track. Even Jamie and the house in Mapua—fit. Like a puzzle, or chainlink, or helix strands.

Chapter Two

"Let's go into Nelson," Jamie beamed.

It was at times like this Anne felt the difference in their ages. She was nearing 40 and he was 25. Sometimes it made it hard for her. Not the sex, but the knowing.

"What do you want to go into town for?"

"I heard from the guy at the gym down by the docks—you know the one with the honesty box and lock with combo that is ALWAYS empty—well he says there's a great windsurfing place. . ."

"What's wrong?"

"It's just I want to take you there. . ."

"Let's go then."

"You mean it? You're going to workout with me?"

"No, you know I won't do that with anyone. I train alone. I'd go windsurfing with you."

I train for Gene

"But Anne—it's kind of weird you know."

"I know. Remember when we first met and you said you were a loner?"

"But that was before I met YOU! I don't want to be alone now—I want to be with you!"

"I understand, it's changed for you and believe me, sweetheart," she took Jamie's face into her hands like Gene had taken hers, "it means more to me than you know that you'd let those walls down for me like that . . ."

I feel sick to my stomach. Hold it together… just a little more… don't blow it…DO YOUR JOB!!!!

". . . but I'm a lot older than you are."

"What's that got to do with it?"

"Everything."

"That's not an answer."

"It's all the answer I can give."

"That's not fair!"

"I never promised fair. Now are we going to go into Nelson or what?"

He sighed, "I guess so."

Later. . .

"See Anne, isn't this a blast!"

He was right. It is fun. I do love watching him. The energy he has—it reminds me—once, so long ago. Look at those muscles! My God, he's built. All the girls see it too. It's not fair to him to be with me. He needs to have someone his own age. Someone to love—who can love him back. . .

"Hey Anne, stop daydreaming and get your butt over here on this windsurfer!"

He's going to kill me. . .no, that's right

"Okay, you get up like this alright?"

"Since when did you become an expert?"

"Since we've been living here six months and I go down to the bay nearly every day to do it!"

Six months. No it can't be already. SHIT! I have to get those tests.

"AHHHHH"

"Just let go Anne," Jamie was yelling while running down the beach, "Just let go and drop!"

Anne felt the wind taking her, suddenly. One moment she was water: the next sky and everything quiet everything as it was could be no other way.

The rockpier came closer. Waves crashed their dulcimer rhythm that lulled Anne's feet to believing in glidingwood—would break, crumble—tumbling water. . .then Jamie cradling her head to his chest, ""Sweetiesweetieyoualright? Tell me you're alright!"

"I'm alright."

"Thank God!"

Anne smiled, "Thought you didn't believe in God."

Jamie kissed her cheek, "You've made me believe in a lot of things."

Oh God! God forgive me. Gene

[NIGHThome]

Jamie made Anne her favorite Kiwi food, chicken croquettes. Well, he hadn't exactly made them; he'd stopped at a little shop on their way home from Nelson and had bought them from the Dutch family that ran the shop.

"I tried making Trifle today," Jamie said, handing Anne her plate.

"Oh yeah, how'd it turn out?"

"After dinner you can be the judge."

Oh boy-can't wait! I still remember the beef-somosa affair. I was on the pot for days! Sometimes I wonder who's doing what to whom.

"I'm glad you like to cook."

"Well," Jamie said, "I don't know as I like to cook as much as I like to bake."

"Yeah, I figured. That's why I've packed on a stone since we moved."

"YOU HAVE???"

Jamie danced around like a little fair exclaiming, "WHY I NEVER NOTICED!"

Anne stood up, "What's THAT supposed to mean?"

"You know you could always come work out with me—see," he said, pointing to a six-packed abdomen.

Anne reared off and punched him in between the squares.

"HEY! That hurt!"

"See—I don't need to workout with you."

His face changed.

"What?"

"Nothing."

"Come on, there's no use in holding out. You know you'll tell me eventually."

"Yeah, I know, I'm such a wimp when it comes to YOU Anne."

"Is that what this is all about?"

"That?"

"Me being strong?"

"No—being cruel isn't being strong. Being able to build things, to grow things, to move things—that's strong."

Anne was silent, for the second time.

Chapter Three

"We're preparing for our descent. The local time is 10:15 and the current temperature is 85 degrees. Please return to your seat, fasten your seatbelts, and return your tray into the upright position. On behalf of . . ."

"I've never been to L.A."

"Is that a bad thing?"

Jamie shook his head and smiled, "No, but it's kind of nice to be able to say I've at least been here."

Anne nodded.

Jamie was watching the sky out the window when he reached for Anne's hand. She noticed that when his skin touched hers a tremor began. She'd been feeling them more and more.

"Hey," she said to Jamie, "Do you feel that?"

"Oh it's nothing. Just turbulence."

It's begun

They took a cab.

"Cool!"

"What?"

"I always wanted to go to a university."

Anne laughed. "Yeah, well they're not all they're cracked up to be."

He nudged her arm, "Oh yeah, you a college grad?"

Anne nodded.

"No shit!"

"No shit."

"Damn, woman! You have some serious secrets."

If you only knew

"Hi Anne."

Jamie raised his crooked eyebrows and whispered, "They know your name?"

"They should. This is my 16th PET scan."

"What's a pet scan?"

"Positron emission tomography. Everyone calls it PET."

He winked, "You're my pet."

"Oh shut up," Anne whispered, but kissed his cheek.

"We're ready for you."

As Anne walked into the room Jamie called out, "What are they scanning you for?"

"Dopamine."

***

"Anne Whiting."

Anne followed the technician into the MRI room.

"You sure get a lot of these."

"Yeah," Anne sighed, "can't be too careful nowadays."

"You got Parkinson's disease?"

"Yeah."

"How old are you?"

"37."

"Damn, Girl, I'm sorry."

"Don't be. Sometimes disease is a blessing from God. . . by the way,

can I get a set of earplugs. I hate the noise."

"No problem, Sweetie."

*Someone used to call me 'sweetie.' I remember I really liked them.
Oh GOD! I can't remember. Who was it? Think...THINK! Think
darn it AnneYourbrain'sgone all to mushIhope it'sworthit.*

***

"We'll be landing in Hawaii. . . thank you. . ."

"By the way," Anne whispered into Jamie's ear {it smelled of him: his sweet athletic sex she'd gotten used to} "you smell good—enough to EAT," and she touched the tip of her tongue to inner edge of his ear's ridge.

"Easy, girl! We're just about ready to land and we've got a LONG ass flight back home."

"Really?"

"Yeah. What? Something like 20 hours?"

"Oh. I guess I better not tell you. . ."

"Tell me what?"

"that I'm not wearing any panties and. . ."

"STOP!" Jamie re-adjusted himself in his seat.

". . .I put some warm vanilla just where you like to take a taste and. . ."

"AND??!!" Jamie sucked in air hard.

". . . I'm in the mood for EVERYTHING!"

"Annie, you're not playing fair!"

Anne leaned back, arched and displayed her neck. He loved kissing her neck, sucking her skin into his mouth.

"And. . .I have a surprise for you."

"You mean there's MORE!"

"OHHH yeah!"

"Tell me! Tell me!"

"How would you like to spend a couple weeks here in Hawaii?"

Chapter 4

The PET and MRI results came to Mapua.

Thanks Dr. Vald

Dr. Vald had been Gene's doctor so when Anne came to him, after Gene's death, showing signs of paranoia over contracting Parkinson's disease and multiple sclerosis he handled her differently than he would have his other patients.

After all, he and Gene were more than doctor and patient—they'd grown up together. In fact, they'd been best friends.

Truth be told, Dr. Vald didn't want to medicate Anne; he knew what the potential consequences were of having certain medications on one's permanent health record.

He was, therefore, quite relieved when Anne brought to her appointment copies of studies she'd found—studies by legitimate researchers from credible universities—citing cases of parkinsonism between husbands and wives. It was all he needed to go along with her request: 2x PET scans per year and 2x MRIs per year/every year—indefinitely.

If this will set her mind at ease, without meds, then it's worth it. Besides, I know she can afford it. If this is how she wants to spend Gene's money—I can figure a lot worse ways people try to cope with the kind of loss she's suffering.

Imagine his surprise then—after her first year's PET scan and MRI had pictured a perfectly normal brain—when Anne's consequential tests confirmed not only Early Onset Parkinsonism but multiple sclerosis.

When Dr. Vald asked her to go to one of the US's top medical facilities for a full diagnostic work-up she declined: she'd been that route with Gene…and the doctors had not listened.

She did, once, find one: he confessed (off record of course) that even if Gene's parkinsonism had been caused by some toxic exposure to hexavalent chromium that there was nothing science and medicine had to offer him with regard to treatment/management. She determined then—however—that she would have much to offer…all of them.

***

Have just reviewed and compared all previous PET to current

PET. Results=: proof of diminishing dopamine neurons at predictable

intervals based on CrVI exposure.

I am now introducing final exposure route IV (intravenous) at

½ ML 1x per day in addition to those previously/currently being

employed:

½ ML IM (intramuscular injection) 1x per day [at various sights
including thigh, gluteals, shoulder, abdomen]
1 milligram capsule 3x per day
1 milligram capsule particulate via inhalant 1 x per day
CrVI (sodium dichromate)/ DMSO (a topical transdermal)
compounded at concentrations 9%/10% PLO GE

Please refer to previous notes for dates of introduction for each

of the above-mentioned hexavalent chromium additions and cross-

reference with corresponding PET/MRI (all of which are dated

accordingly).

You will find that all the data supports prior body of

knowledge regarding the toxicity, carcinogenicity, teratrogenicity, and

DNA mutagenicity studies previously published which can be verified

by tissue samples.

The enclosed physician records I give to public domain. ANYONE interested (not just researchers and physicians but the general public, university students, wives and husbands who have found their loved ones suffering) I give COMPLETE ACCESS to ALL my personal information. My ENTIRE purpose is to give what would NOT be given, freely, to me—knowledge.

I don't know if there will be additional entries. I suspect (if any) there will not be many. But I did find out one thing, Gene, why. Why, when they put you on that [ACE-inhibitor] you felt like a million bucks after just one dose (when it was supposed to take at least 5 days to build up in your system). It was because they didn't know that the [ACE-inhibitor] ALSO inhibited {Na-K-ATPase}.

Remember, you asked me about that letter from Dr. Puruk about why I was going on about magnesium and what did it have to do with chromium and I didn't have the answer then?

Well, I have it now. Because of the CrVI you had been overproducing {Na-K-ATPase} and when you took that [ACE-inhibitor] for your cholesterol/blood pressure (remember it didn't lower it at all) well your body FINALLY got to have a normal ionic balance. I know this because I, too, experienced the same phenomenon. There, my love, there is your answer.

I'm just so terribly sorry it has come too late.

Dr. Kovich looked up from the binder of Anne Whiting and stared, blank-faced at the young man who'd brought it to him.

"What am I supposed to do with this?"

"You're the expert RIGHT?"

"I. . . uh. . . this is not. . . I."

"Is that what a college degree gets you? Man, I'm glad I didn't go. Thanks for your time. I got more people on my list to see."

Jamie reached for the folder but Dr. Kovich pulled it to his chest like a dog to a bitch.

"HOLD on a minute. You come in here cold and with THIS! And expect me to, I don't KNOW WHAT? What do you expect me to do?"

"I don't expect a damn thing! The only woman I've ever loved is dead, on ice, waiting for some EXPERT. . ." Jamie spat that word like acid, "like YOU? To prove what I always knew."

"What?"

"That she was FUCKING AMAZING!"

Dr. Kovich looked at the young man. Looked at the folder. "How many folders did you say there are?"

"You college guys! I told you already, a couple hundred."

Jamie then held out his notecards and read:

"The job is: head researcher at the Gene Whiting Library for the Advancement of Chromium Studies in Ashland, Oregon. In exchange for accepting this position. . ."

Jamie mumbled under his breath, ". . .makin' more than I ever did doin' an HONEST day's work. . . "

". . .you will be allowed to conduct ALL scientific study necessary on the body of Anne Whiting."

Dr. Kovich leaned back in his chair.

"Anne asked me to give you this if you didn't jump at this offer."

As Jamie handed him the sealed letter Jamie growled, "idiot."

Dr. Kovich squinted his eyes.

Dear Dr. Kovich,

By now you already know my name. I, however, have known yours for a long time now. You began your studies on hexavalent chromium nearly 25 years ago. I've studied your career. As well as your colleagues'. I have chosen you for two reasons: first, you have no life other than science. I knew you would, on some level then, understand my own dedication to this endeavor. Because…the only life I ever knew—Gene—died. Second, you are a good man.

I have watched your work be downplayed because it told the truth and others' work get headlines because it lied.

You and I both know that hexavalent chromium is big business. It's in everything from computers to toasters. It's even in the dyed-canvas tents of our military/service men/women. It's a multi-billion dollar industry.

So a few people die, right? COST/BENEFIT=ends justify means. Besides, everyone gets cheaper electricity and OIL. Well murder and lying didn't work for me but I'm not alone: Mathew

Whosoever therefore shall break one of the least commandments,
And shall teach men so,
He shall be called the least in the kingdom of heaven:
But whosoever shall do and teach them,
The same shall be called great in the kingdom of heaven.
One life mattered—to me:

AND THE KING SHALL ANSWER AND SAY UNTO THEM,

VERILY I SAY UNTO YOU,

INASMUCH AS YE HAVE DONE IT UNTO THE LEAST OF MY BRETHREN,

YE HAVE DONE IT UNTO ME.   MATHEW

I suspect you're not a spiritual man but I want you to understand that

YOU have a choice to make just as I did:

CHOICE #1	CHOICE #2
JEREMIAH AND THEY SHALL TEACH NO MORE EVERY MAN HIS NEIGHBOR, AND EVERY MAN HIS BROTHER, SAYING, KNOW THE LORD: FOR THEY SHALL KNOW ME, FROM THE LEAST OF THEM UNTO THE GREATEST OF THEM, SAITH THE LORD: FOR I WILL FORGIVE THEIR INIQUITY, AND I WILL REMEMBER THEIR SIN NO MORE.	JEREMIAH AND I WILL TAKE THE REMNANT OF JUDAH, THAT HAVE SET THEIR FACES TO GO INTO THE LAND OF EGYPT TO SOJOURN THERE, AND THEY SHALL ALL BE CONSUMED, AND FALL IN THE LAND OF EGYPT; THEY SHALL EVEN BE CONSUMED BY THE SWORD AND BY FAMINE: THEY SHALL DIE, FROM THE LEAST EVEN UNTO THE GREATEST, BY THE SWORD AND BY THE FAMINE: AND THEY SHALL BE AN EXECRATION, AND AN ASTONISHMENT, AND A CURSE, AND A REPROACH.

My Dear Dr. Kovich, hexavalent chromium's money is incense burnt

to the false god of industry.

But false gods DO FALL! I give you courage.

Should you accept this position: you will find

senators/representatives (and their families) happy to endorse your

efforts. Mark my word. Anne

Dr. Kovich set the letter down,

Jamie

at

up

looked

and nodded.

pART ii,iii,iv,v...of II

CHEST

Bench:

onetwothreefourfivesixseveneight nine   ten

add tens

onetwothreefourfivesixseveneight nine   ten

add tens

onetwothree fourfive sixseven   eight niiiiinnnneten

add 2 ½ s

one two three four five six seven eight niiiinnnneeeeeee

shit! take off 2 ½ s . Final set. Get it!

onetwothreefourfivesixseveneight nine   ten

Damn, too easy, should have kept the 2 ½ s

NOW: 5 sets10reps:peckdeck/flys/pushups/abs

***

"You sure, luv?"

"Yeah. I'm sure."

"Because I can almost guarantee you at least 10K more if you wait to sell until summer."

"No. In fact, I want you to drop the price. I need a quick sale."

"What's your hurry?"

"I'm going back to the States as soon as this place sells."

"I'm sorry to hear about your wife."

Jamie looked at the real estate agent. He didn't have the heart to correct her mistake, "Me too."

***

BACK

T-Bar Rows:

onetwothreefourfivesixseveneight nine   ten

add ten

onetwothreefourfivesixseveneight nine   ten

add ten

onetwothree fourfive sixseveneightnine ten

add ten

one two three four five six seven eight nine ten

shit! too easy. 25s final set. Get it!

Onetwothreefour fivesix seven eightnine teeeeennnnnn

Damn, that was a good set!

NOW: 5 sets10reps:shrugs/pulldowns/pullups/abs

***

This is crazy. What am I doing? Sure, the money is good. I mean I got my year's salary upfront so it's not about that it's just so weird! I mean this woman. . . she was a NUTTER! Yet . . . if the notebook I have in my hands is ANY indication of her thoroughness throughout the process. . . MY GOD! This is a dream come true! No one in the world has this kind of information available to them. I can finally see. . . albeit through a neophyte's eyes. . . the full power of Cr6. If. . .

"We're preparing our decent into Medford. Thanks for flying. . ."

It sure is small here compared to Boston.

***

SHOULDERS

Military Press:

onetwothreefourfivesixseveneight nine   ten

add fives

onetwothreefourfivesixseveneight nine   ten

pull fives/add tens

onetwothree fourfive sixseven   eight nine ten

add 2 ½ s

one two three four five six seven eiaaaaaaght niiiinnnneeeeeee

take off 2 ½ s . Final set. Get it!

one two three four five six seven eight nine ten

Good.

NOW: 5 sets10reps:reversedumbbellflys/barbellfrontraise/abs

***

"Why are you selling, if you don't mind us asking?"

Jamie was proud of himself that he could tell the difference between the prospective buyer's British accent and that of the Kiwi's.

Looking out the bay window overlooking Mapua's beach he remembered when he and Anne had first come to New Zealand and how it had taken him nearly two weeks before he could make out half of what the newscasters were saying on the Tele.

His brow knit, "My wife died."

Some lies were easier

"I'm so sorry."

The woman's eyes got wide—a child's "is money worth the scares of a haunted Hallow-house."

"She didn't die here."

"Oh?"

"No."

The realtor, who'd been showing the woman's husband the workshop in the basement, came in to find Jamie and the woman dead quiet.

"Well," the realtor piped, "What do you think of the house?"

The husband boomed, "It's great. We'll take it."

The woman looked between Jamie and the realtor and though she never said another word it wasn't difficult to see that Anne's death had touched another life.

***

LEGS

Squat:

onetwothreefourfivesixseveneightnincten

Warm-up doesn't count, do it again with real weight

One two three four five six seven eight nine ten

Too easy. Don't wimp out. add 45s

One two three four   five six   seven

Don't give up keep pushin

eight niiiiinnnneeeee

one more

ten

*damn! That was a tough set. What number was that? Shit...only 2.
add 10s*

okay okay number 3 number 3 get this set GET IT

one two three four five six seven eight nine ten

TOO EASY! That's #3. Add 10s. okay 4-only-one-more-here-we-go

One two three four five six seven   eight   nine

Breathe, dig deep, deeper, PUSH!

ten

*YEAH!
NOW: 5 sets10reps:legextensions/stiff-legged
deadlift/seatedcalves/abs*

***

Nice sign—I hate how people fuck with fonts!

Dr. Kovich put the key Jamie had given him into the lock. The door was unwilling. The metal resilient.

Like the tombs of Egypt!

Finally, after shifting the weight of the door itself just slightly to the left while turning the key, he entered into. . .

My God! What a MESS!

***

ARMS:

1st Biceps+

preacher curls:

onetwothreefourfivesixseveneight nineten
onetwothreefourfivesixseveneight nineten
onetwothreefourfive sixseven   eight niiiiinnnne ten
one two three four five six seven eight niiiinnnneeeten
onetwothreefourfivesixseveneight nine   ten

cable curls:

onetwothreefourfivesixseveneight nineten
onetwothreefourfivesixseveneight nineten
onetwothreefourfive sixseven   eight niiiiinnnne ten
one two three four five six seven eight niiiinnnneeeten
onetwothreefourfivesixseveneight nine   ten

EZ curls:

onetwothreefourfivesixseveneight nineten
onetwothreefourfivesixseveneight nineten
onetwothreefourfive sixseven   eight niiiiinnnne ten
one two three four five six seven eight niiiinnnneeeten
onetwothreefourfivesixseveneight nine   ten

2nd Tricep+

Skull Crunchers:

onetwothreefourfivesixseveneight nineten
onetwothreefourfivesixseveneight nineten
onetwothreefourfive sixseven   eight niiiiinnnne ten
one two three four five six seven eight niiiinnnneeeten
onetwothreefourfivesixseveneight nine   ten

Close-Grip Bench Press on SMITH:

onetwothreefourfivesixseveneight nineten
onetwothreefourfivesixseveneight nineten
onetwothreefourfive sixseven   eight niiiiinnnne ten
one two three four five six seven eight niiiinnnneeeten
onetwothreefourfivesixseveneight nine   ten

Pressdowns:

onetwothreefourfivesixseveneight nineten
onetwothreefourfivesixseveneight nineten

onetwothreefourfive sixseven   eight niiiiinnnne ten
one two three four five six seven eight niiiinnnneeeten
onetwothreefourfivesixseveneight nine   ten
and ABS

***

"You're James R. Pickett?"

"Yes."

"Sign here. . . Good. Here's your check. Thank you for doing

business with us."

"I didn't."

"Huh?"

"Anne did."

"I'm sorry for your loss," the man's monotone scratched in Jamie's ear

because it sounded a thousand years old, "but . . . with this kind of

money a young guy like you can get a real start if you know what I

mean." The middle-aged insurance salesman with nicotine-stained

middle finger winked.

I wanna knock those front teeth in

"Yeah. Okay."

REST DAY:

***

First thing's first. . .

Laptop in hand, Dr. Ted Kovich typed:

"Initial Inventory of Gene Whiting Library for the Advancement of

Chromium Studies in Ashland, Oregon are as follows:

One corpse (Anne Whiting) donated exclusively to the research of the G.W. Library

150 binders marked Scientific Research
150 binders marked Personal Observation

Texts by title:

"Molecular Biology and Toxicology of Metals;"

Good taste in books!

"A Guide to the Elements 2nd Edition; . . .

***

CHEST DAY= 2HOURS

***

On the short plane ride from Nelson, New Zealand to Auckland Jamie thought about the last time he and Anne had made that flight together. It was just after their vacation had ended in Hawaii.

Why did you do it Annie?

Napali coast flashed into his mind. Those twelve miles would have taken him maybe two days by himself but took them nearly 6. Anne struggled.

He worried. She'd been fatiguing so easy and she'd always been as strong as two regular guys. He noticed—on those trails above the sea—that her muscles had atrophied. There were rashes of patches over parts—her left shoulder, her right thigh and the back of her neck. They blistered when she'd sweat.

He walked behind or beside her as if a ghost.

Even when they stopped and watched the clear ocean from the cliffs Anne wasn't really there. Her face seemed hard stone—like part of Calalau's beach.

That night, in their yellow two-man tent:

"Are you alright, Anne?"

"Sure. Are you alright?"

Jamie rolled to his back, staring at the darkening tent seams.

"Annie, I'd like to know what's going on with you."

She smiled, "What do you mean?"

He turned his head and looked her straight in the eye, "I may not be the smartest guy but I'm not stupid!"

Her brow wrinkled, "I've never thought you were stupid."

"Then what! What is it?"

"What's what?"

"Why won't you tell me what's happening?"

Anne touched his cheek. His whiskers prickled her fingers and she smiled, "My beautiful Jamie, you deserve so much goodness."

Tears came to his eyes because it felt like she was saying goodbye. It felt. . .and he managed, "I want you. . ."

"I'm dying."

***

BACK DAY=2HOURS

***

At his desk, Ted Kovich opened the first journal marked 1.

VERY basic information was found. This was true of all the folders

marked 2-20 and 22 too:

What's Parkinson's disease?

blahblahblah

What's dopamine?

blahblah

What are the symptoms/treatments available?

blah

There were schematics of neurotransmitters and their

corresponding enzymes. Drawings of brains. Drawings of cells.

Things one would learn in their first year of biochemistry at a small

college (or advanced high school). Nothing stood out as exceptionally

interesting therefore much irritated Dr. Ted Kovich.

*Why am I here? Have I made a terrible mistake? No. I have what she
didn't. I know what I need to know and she gave me what I needed to
prove it. Still, it is torture to read these babblings. Every novice
thinks they're Einstein. That's why I HATED teaching! Those kids!*

They think they're so brilliant barking out theories older than I am and acting like they're the latest greatest! Well, I'd better get back to it. Only, I can't look at these anymore tonight. Maybe the Personal Observations will prove more interesting

PO Binder 1

According to the EPA's Sodium Dichromate Listing Background

Document of August 2000:

66% sodium dichromate dihydrate (sodium bichromate or sodium bichromate dihydrate) for chromic acid manufacture
13% leather tanning
9% chromic oxide production
6% pigments manufacture
6% in the manufacture of other things such as:
     wood preservatives
     paints
     drilling muds
     metal treatment agents

Also—
metal finishing industry for coating base metals
decorative plating
conversion coatings
metal coloring compounds

Chromic oxide mixed with:
     Copper
     Aluminum
     And other oxides

Is used as a catalyst in organic reactions of:
Hydrogenation
Dehydrogenation
Polymerization
Catalytic reforming

Chrome Sulfate=leather tanning

Sodium dichromate=pigment industry. Lead chromate used in manufacturing:

Paints
Printing inks
Paper coloring
FLOOR coverings!

Other chromium compounds containing:

Zinc
Strontium
Barium

Form pigments with corrosion-inhibiting qualities

FOR PAINT PRIMERS for METAL

Chromic green oxide (another sodium dichromate derived pigment) is:

Resistant to:

Light
Heat
Acids
Alkalis

(NOTE: THIS SOUNDS TO ME LIKE IT COULD REALLY FUCK YOU UP IF YOU GOT IT IN YOUR BODY!!!)

And is used in:

Rubber
Roofing
Shingles
Cement
Ceramics
Chemical-resistant paints.

Sodium dichromate also used in textile dying or producing the dyes themselves.

Also used in:

OIL WELL DRILLING muds

(because sodium dichromate creates soluble chromates for corrosion control and chrome lignosulfates for deflocculation and thinning agents which help control drilling mud viscosity).

Manufacturing:

PHOTOGRAPHIC FILMS

FLAVORS
ESSENTIAL OILS
SACCHARIN

PHARMACEUTICALS

PYROTECHNICS
EXPLOSIVES
SAFETY MATCHES
CHROME GLUES

ADHESIVES
WOOD STAINS

POISON FLY PAPER

PROCESS ENGRAVING AND LITHOGRAPHY
SYNTHETIC PERFUMES
CHROME ALUM MANUFACTURE
ALLOYS
CERAMIC PRODUCTS
DEPOLARIZERS IN DRY CELL BATTERIES
BLEACHING FATS AND WAXES

(NOTE: FROM WHAT I CAN READ BETWEEN THE LINES IN THIS DOCUMENT CR6 IS AN INDUSTRY STANDARD THAT IS ALREADY BEING ACKNOWLEDGED [IN 2000] AS TOXIC AND BEING SUGGESTED TO FIND ALTERNATIVES FOR WOOD PRESERVATION. SOUNDS A BIT LIKE LEAD (PB) IN THE 1950S. PAY ATTENTION TO WHAT IT'S SAYING: CR6 EFFECTS POLARITY, FATS, AND BONDS WITH OTHER METALS. HOW DOES THIS RELATE TO PARKINSONISM?)

Where is she going with this?

***

SHOULDER DAY=2HOURS

***

Jamie didn't look out the airplane window once. His eyes caressed each and every word, over and over again, like a starving person who's given a promise of food.

"My Dear Jamie,

This journal is for you and you alone. All the others I hope you have already shipped to the library. They are for others to see. This one is between you and me. I have so much to tell you and, I fear, very little time. You see I too once loved as—deeply.

I only pray you will see my words spin a cautionary tale. One can love such that it hurts everyone it touches."

He thought of the last time they'd made love...on Napali beach.

"You can't die!"

"Everyone dies. You're young, that's all. It seems dramatic when you're young."

Jamie grabbed Anne's face in his hands, trembling, as if moved by a great violence,

"You're young too!"

She laughed, "You're sweet."

"I mean it DAMN it!"

He kissed her hard. Not like love. Not like passion.

Like mouth-to-mouth.   And he didn't stop. He pulled her shirt up to her neck, pushed her panties aside and entered her.

"Remember, in Hawaii, when we made love? I want you to know that I realized something that night. I felt your body melt and your weight relax against my chest, my stomach, my legs. I smelled your hair and it smelled like the sea.

I want you to know that—then—I knew I loved you.

I'm so sorry for all of this, my dearest Jamie, for although I've loved you as best I could. I was too broken. . . and it wasn't

your fault."

"Would you like something to drink?" The flight attendant asked.

"No thank you."

Jamie didn't look up. He didn't want anyone to see his eyes.

***

LEG DAY=2HOURS

***

Final Page: Binder 1

According to UC Davis (envtox.ucdavis.edu.chromium6) "Although a

drinking water standard has been established, long-term human health

effects from consuming water containing more than 50 mg/L of

hexavalent chromium have not been identified."

(NOTE: That will be the standard ratio. What is a liter? How many

liters in a gallon? How many grams of Cr6 will I need to inject into a

5-gallon water bottle?)

Ted looked up from the Anne's journal and scanned the room.

In the corner stood a 5-gallon water dispenser.

Note to self <DON'T use the water cooler>

***

ARM DAY=2HOURS

***

"How much is a monthly membership?"

The guy looked Jamie up and down. He did that to everyone who came into his gym, "50."

Jamie looked around.

Power-racks. Smiths. 100-lb plates. Hardcore gym.

"You gonna' pay or just stand around gawkin'?"

Jamie laughed. He handed the guy a fifty-dollar bill. "By the way, what's your name?"

"Bill."

I remember you. You're Anne's Bill

"You know Anne Whiting?"

Bill looked Jamie up and down again but with different eyes, "Why ya' askin'?"

"She was my wife."

Bill raised his eyebrows, "No kiddin'? I never thought she'd hook up again after Gene. How's she doin'?"

"She's dead."

"No shit?"

"No shit."

***

REST DAY

***

Although parts of the library appeared in order it seemed to Dr. Ted Kovich that much was in need to be done by the way of organization and he was only too glad to set Anne Whiting's "personal observations" and "scientific binders" aside for some route moving of one thing from its place to another.

Truth told—he hadn't really explored the entire "library" either. Something about the place made him feel a little like he'd always felt (growing up with his family; he liked science: his family liked sports and drinking beer)—an unwelcome stranger.

He went into the dissection room. It smelled unlike any other lab he'd been in.

What is that smell? Like road-kill mixed with pine-scented cleaning solution—no, like rancid jerky and dead flowers—no, I can't place that, that smell!

On a silver table lay the body of Anne Whiting. She was covered in tradition's white sheet displaying her carcass' outline: the shape of her nose, her breasts, her knee^caps and toes slightly falling outward in a V.

Ted pulled her covering aside. It wasn't the first time he'd seen a dead body, though for dissection it was customary for the head to be removed prior to students being allowed to flay formaldehyde-flesh with careless scalpels. He looked at her cloudy, baby-blue%dead-eyes and waited. For what? Not even he knew.

***

CHEST DAY

***

"Hello. Ashland Land Management."

"I'd like to look at one of your listings."

"Great. Have you already filled out an application?"

"No."

"Well you'll need to come to the office, fill out an application, we'll do a credit check and then we can schedule an appointment to view the property."

"You mean I can't just go look at it to see if I even want to fill out an application?"

"No sir. You must go through the application process first. Oh, and I almost forgot, there's a $50 application fee."

"Clever."

"Excuse me?"

"Nothing. What's your name?"

"I'm Jen Stell."

"Hi Jen. My name's Jamie. I'll see you in a few minutes then. By the way, if I like the place I'll pay the year's rent upfront—in cash."

"Okay Jamie. I look forward to meeting you." Jen hung up the phone.

Some people! What nerve! Like 'I'll pay a year ahead in cash' as if he's a big deal or something. Man, I wish I had that kind of money to be able to do that. A year's rent—ahead. I'm still trying to figure out how to pay my share of rent for my friend's couch. And I nearly fucked up again! Thank God Mr. Jones didn't hear me. He'd have been all over me. I can't stand him. I KNOW what he's thinking when he comes down on me—reprimanding me like I'm 2 years old—while looking at my breasts. I wish, for once, a man would see me for me and not for my body.

"Jen!"

"Yes Mr. Jones."

"I need to have you show this man the house on Granite Street."

From out of Mr. Jone's office walked the most beautiful man she'd ever seen through her 0just-being-eighteen0 eyes.

146

He wasn't too tall. Not short. Perfect. His hair was between strawberry-blonde and fawn and his body—

WOW!!! He's GORGEOUS!

"Hi, I'm Jamie. I believe we spoke earlier," he said, stretching out his hand to Jen's.

"Hi. . . I. . . uh. . . am Jen. . .uh"

Mr. Jones watched his newest property manager/secretary/summer help stumble all over herself and, looking at the young man, could understand why.

But understanding whys doesn't make people feel better. At least not Mr. Jones who'd found balding, fifty pounds over weight, and relying more and more on 'performance' enhancers when it came to making love with his wife near-intolerable.

"Jen. Do you THINK you could show this man the house. . . SOMETIME today?"

"Oh I'm sorry Mr. Jones," the young girl scrambled with a stack of papers on her desk. "You'll have to fill out the application and have a back…"

"NO!" Mr. Jones interrupted, "just SHOW him the house NOW."

Jen raised her eyebrows and her eyes got big, "If you say so Mr. Jones."

He stormed into his office, mumbling "I say so."

Jamie watched the fat man shut the door behind him. He'd seen his kind all his life. Men who hated men who had what they wanted.

"Hey," Jamie said in a voice softer than any he'd used in months, "Give me the application."

The girl, near to tears, said, "No. I can't. Let's just go to the property. I can't lose this job."

"Okay."

"You can follow me," she said.

When Jen clutched her Chinese-made briefcase to her fleshed chest she accidentally rattled the ringed-key she'd taken from the hooked-wall where penetrating keys to doors of houses waited for people to enter.

***

BACK DAY

***

I don't like these folders being here. They should be—over here. . .

Ted Kovich carried Anne Whiting's journals from the

bookshelves nearest the front door to the bookshelves nearest the

office he'd assumed for himself.

That process took an hour.

Office supplies. . . okay—they're in the closet here. That's alright.
Bathroom—Nasty! Need: toilet paper, toilet bowl cleaner/toilet brush
and...a blue-toilet-water-smelly thing.

Throughout the building the doctor found bits and pieces of a

life that had nothing what-so-ever to do with chemistry.

These things need to be cleared out. Where to put them? I shouldn't
just throw them away, but they can't stay where they are. A closet
maybe? A storage room? There was one I think in the back. Ah, yes.
There.

He carried framed photos, framed certificates, framed business

licenses: WHITING'S LEATHER TANNERY

Now the smell makes sense

Then he found, in a drawer of a small writing desk near the

main front door, a small black leather-bound book with gold-leafed pages. It was locked with a heart-shaped lock that wrapped round the book's spine and bound it shut with leather.

There were no words on the outside. There was, however, a compulsion Ted felt to find a way into those golden pages. In the office he placed it on the desk, next to Anne Whiting's (P)ersonal (O)bservations.

This place is certainly surreal.

Dr. Kovich found one remedy for his kwashiorkerstomached-expectations…busy hands.

I've been paid. No one is here. And if I take time to organize this place how I need it to be for my research, I can't be faulted.

Yet, that little book…

[sweeping]—[ordering tools]—[ordering tools]

kept shimmering his brain [ordering equipment] and he found himself longing to set science aside for finding a way to penetrate the flesh-lock[-ed glitter of it].

SHOULDER DAY

As she unlocked the door she turned to look at Jamie's face and
smiled, "This is a great house."

"Oh yeah, why?"

"Well. . . " assuming a stage/dramatic role she flung the door wide to
an open floor-planned house of wood, tiles, stained glass windows,
island kitchen with custom cabinets, built-ins, sauna (complete with its
own shower), a hot tub, a second bath with double-headed [walk-in]
shower. ". . .it is the most unique place I've ever seen."

Jamie looked at the girl's eyes. He found himself feeling. . .
something. . .like excitement—or infection.

"I'll take it," he said flatly.

"Great! Here's the application form. You can fill it out now or drop it
by the office, oh, and I'll need your application fee."

"I'll fill it out now if you don't mind waiting."

She pushed her lower lip out and looked at her watch. It was her lunch
hour. "Not at all."

They went out on the wrap-around wooden deck steps and Jamie wrote for a total of five minutes.

"There," he said, handing the papers back to Jen.

She raised her eyebrows, "You're done already?"

"Yep."

She looked at the application form:

Date_____
Name: James R. Picket
Address: Columbia Hotel
Phone: Columbia Hotel
Last rental/residence: I owned my home in New Zealand. . .

"Oh I've always wanted to go to New Zealand! What's it like?"

Jamie smiled and shook his head, "Pretty nice."

"Oh yeah, I bet it's wonderful there. I've seen pictures, you know, on the television. It looks like paradise."

Jamie turned quietly gray.

Jen noticed.

"I'm sorry, I shouldn't babble like that." She returned to the application:

Employment (last five years): Security Guard, Capitol Building, Washington D.C.

Length of Employment: 15 years

Reason for Leaving: Moved to New Zealand

Current Employer: Self (independently wealthy)

"Oh."

"Is there a problem?"

"No. No sir."

Jen stood up and nervously brushed her lap as if it had invisibly gotten dirty.

"I am sorry I went on and on."

"No problem. So when can I move into the house?"

"I'll take these back to Mr. Jones right away. I'm sure you can move in ASAP."

"May I follow you to the office? I'd like to pay the year's rent now."

"Uh. . .sure."

Once inside the safety of her little hatch-backed car Jen exhaled. She'd never met a truly wealthy person before. Everyone she'd ever known was as poor as she was. Living in a small college town her level of exposure to the financial upper echelon had been relatively deprived.

***

LEG DAY

***

The Gene Whiting Library had been 'renovated,' or so Ted was told while he was still in Boston. The position included an apartment (within the library) for the researcher—rent-free. After being scalped on rent in Boston for years that sounded good to Ted.

Yet often times what something sounds like is not, upon realization, what one has hoped for; Ted decided he needed a separate place to rent—if only to escape the stench.

ARM DAY/REST/CHESTDAY/BACK/DAY/SHOULDER DAY

***

"Hi Bill."

"Hi Jamie. What'cha' workin' today?"

"Legs."

"Good. Leg-days are good days."

"I agree."

"Hey," Bill called out to Jamie as he was loading 45s onto the bar, "You wanna' work out with me and the guys sometime?"

Jamie looked at the old man. He was built, that was for sure, but he had a different reason for saying yes. Jamie had known of Anne's Bill from Anne and he secretly hoped, through Bill, he could know her better. He agreed.

"Okay then. We start at 5 in the morning. If you're late. Don't bother comin' in or comin' back."

"Thanks."

Bill laughed. "Don't thank me yet, kid. Let's see how thankful you are AFTER the workout."

***

"Ashland Land Management."

"Hi. My name is Dr. Ted Kovich."

"Hello Dr. Kovich, how can I help you?"

"I need to find a month-to-month."

"What kind of price range are you looking for?"

"Cheap."

"Understandably. First, you'll need to come down to the office and fill out an application. We do a credit check and require a $50 application fee. When you're here you can look at the listings we have."

"Okay. Is there a certain time I should come?"

"No. Any time is fine."

"And with whom am I speaking?"

"My name is Jen Stell."

"Okay. Thank you Ms. Stell. I'll see you shortly."

"You're welcome Dr. Kovich. I look forward to it."

***

ARMS

***

"Hello, is Jen Stell there?"

"Speaking."

"Hi, this is Jamie—you know you showed me the house on Granite
Street—. . . "

As if I could forget YOU

". . . —and I was wondering if you might be able to help me with
something."

"I'll do my best."

"I don't know my way around this town. . . (he mumbled—not that it's
very big that's for sure). . . and I need to get some furniture and stuff.
Do you think you could put me in touch with someone who might be
able to show me around and help buy stuff—you know, get on my
feet. . ."

Oh my gosh! Oh my gosh! Be cool. Don't jump! Okay, breathe,
breathe
". . . because I've got some projects I need done and I'll pay them for
their work."

"Uh. . . if you want I'd be hap—py to help you."

"Oh I wouldn't want to bother you with that. I just thought since you rent people houses and stuff that you'd know people who could help with moving and stuff. Settling in, getting stuff done."

"Really!. . ."

Easy girl. Easy. Tone it down.

". . . really, I'd love to help. And you don't have to pay me."

"I couldn't do that."

"Please, it's my pleasure. Besides, I love to shop."

Oh dammit! I shouldn't have said THAT!

"Good, because I hate to. So when can you start?"

"You mean help?"

"I mean start working as my assistant."

"JEN! A guy wants to look at that little Main Street house. Get over there right now—he's already there and waiting."

"Okay Mr. Jones. I'm on my way."

"You mean like a full-time job?"

"Yeah."

"Oh, I don't know about that. . . "

"Are you gone yet? What the heck are you doing?"

"I'm just getting the keys. I'm leaving just now."

"Can I think about that?"

"Come by after you show the house," he paused, "or tomorrow—and tell me your answer."

"JEN!!!"

***

CHEST

***

"Hi."

"Hi. I'm Dr. Kovich."

"We spoke. I'm Jen."

"Hi Jen. Thanks for coming out to show me this house."

"No problem."

She opened the front door to one of the smallest houses she'd ever seen. It made her roommate's apartment look grand.

"The square footage is just-a-little-under-600."

Ted eyed the room and walked through the only doorway into a closet-sized. . .

"bedroom?"

"Yeah," Jen laughed. So did Ted.

"I'd say about 50-under 600 at least."

"Yeah," she smiled, but lowered her eyes to the

neon-orange'^'^'^shag carpet.

My God. She's beautiful! Her eyes are like liquid blue-green algae and her lips like crimson calendula extracted from pulp paste!

"And this," he said pointing to the toilet and sink standing in the corner, "must be the deluxe bathroom."

She giggled.

Her cheeks are like peaches and her breasts like succulent aloe pods

"And the rent is cheap," Jen piped, getting back to business, "and, honestly, Dr. Kovich, you won't find cheaper in this town. Believe me, I've tried."

"Really?" He asked, drawling out his L and Y.

"It's a college town."

"Oh. . . and you? You go to college here?"

"I'm starting Fall."

"Great! Congratulations. Do you know what you want to . . ."

be when you grow up?

". . .study?"

"Art."

He grinned.

Perfect. Ask her.

"Would you like to get a cup of coffee?"

Jen looked at her watch, "I would like to but. . ."

"Perhaps another time?"

"Sure."

***

BACK

***

"You're early."

"Always."

"Hey guys..."

Five guys of varying size turned their eyes to Jamie.

"...I'd like you to meet Jamie," Bill said.

Like a barbershop quintet, "Hi Jamie:" Rocko, Steve, Max, Ty and Jerry.

Jamie waved.

"Okay you bums, let's get to work."

Two hours of arms. Two hours of little chit-chats about this-and-that: the president, the war, the crappy economy, about who was screwing whom in town and who'd gotten divorced because of it.

Two hours Jamie listened and nodded, smiled and waited and not a word, rather the word, he'd been waiting for: Anne.

***

SHOULDER

***

BEENGGBONG BINGBONG

I've always loved this house

"Come in."

"Hi."

"Hi. I'd ask you to sit down but," he waved his hand like a gameshow

hostess, "no seats."

"I'll take the job."

"I figured as much. Don't you want to know how much?"

"How much what?"

"Wellll. . . furniture, to spend, your salary?"

"Oh yeah, yes, I mean. This is all so weird for me. I mean I've never

got a job like this. Anyway. . .

SHUT UP! Shut up! Stop babbling!

"Okay then, let's start with your salary. How much do you want?"

This is a trick question. Okay what did they say in Career's Class, dammit! I wish I'd paid more attention. OH! Never say how much you want

"I don't know."

"You don't know how much you want to get paid?"

"You decide."

"Fifty cents."

Jen's eyes got big as saucers

"Just kidding. What did you make at the property management

place?"

Straightening her spine, "I'm not going to say. . . I mean do you really

have to know."

Gosh it wasn't very much that's for sure

"No, just tell me what double-it is and that can be what I pay you.

Now I'll need you to help me with several projects. First, furnishing

this house: I don't like a lot of clutter okay?"

"Okay. $16.36."

"Excuse me?"

"Double my wage you said."

"Oh, that. Sure, that's. . ."

"Oh shit, wait. . . I so suck at math. . . it's $16.32."

". . .fine. Let's say $17 an hour and call it good alright?"

"Are you serious?"

You know I wonder if this guy is gay. He hasn't once looked at me in THAT way and yet he's offering me this job as his 'assistant' and. . .

"Uh, Jen?"

"Yes, sorry."

Jamie smiled. It was something he'd noticed doing moreso…around her.

***

LEGS

***

Meanwhile, at the Gene Whiting Library for Chromium:

"Listen, I'm glad you're here."

"Oh yeah, why's that Doc?"

"Call me Ted or Dr. Kovich please."

"Okay. . . Dr. Kovich."

"Well, it's about Mrs. Whiting's body."

"What about it?"

"It's degrading."

"Come again!"

"I mean. . .necrosis after death is normal. Most bodies are, in some way, preserved usually with chemicals but, per Mrs. Whiting's strict request, hers wasn't chemically altered at all. Therefore it is, in fact, rotting."

"I thought that's why it's damn-near frozen. To keep it from doing that."

"Well keeping it cold slows down the process but it doesn't halt it."

"So what are you going to do?"

"Me? What am I going to do? Well, I can tell you that I can't do what I know has to be done all by myself. Not in time."

"Time for what?"

"Before the tissues are compromised."

"Speak English!"

"If we don't get the samples NOW then they'll be ruined. Like spoilt meat, okay? You can keep bologna in the refrigerator for a long time but once it's gone off, well that's all she wrote."

"Don't be a son-of-a-bitch! That's Annie you're talking about in there. Have some respect!"

"Okay, I'm sorry. Sometimes, well a lot of times, I don't communicate things to 'people' well. The point is I need a staff and I need some highly specialized equipment as of yesterday. Do you understand?"

"Do what you need to do. Just keep the costs down as low as you can alright?"

For the first time Ted looked at Jamie as a human being trying to do something. Just like he was trying to do something and neither of them had a realistic grasp upon Something's throat.

"I'll do my best," the doctor replied.

"Oh, and I hired a personal assistant. . .Ted," Jamie called out as he was leaving, "she'll be working at the library as well."

Great. Just what I need. Something else to look after. Now. . .who in the hell am I going to convince to come out here and help me.

Dr. Ted Kovich called associates, superiors, Department heads, private researchers. . .

NOTHING! What the FUCK am I supposed to do?

His fingers ached from dialing. Then the door opened.

It's her. How did she find me? Oh, my application! Yes!!! My lucky day!

"Well HELLLOOOO!"

"Hiiii. . . Dr.?

"Kovich!"

"Yes, that's right."

"What are you doing here?"

"I work for Jamie. I'm his new personal assistant."

SHIT

"Oh."

"So. . .he says you need some help here."

And what the FUCK is someone like you supposed to do to help ME???

"Unless you can somehow manage to put together a team of researchers specializing in biomarkers. . ."

"Have you tried the biology department?"

"Uh. . .no."

Jen smiled.

***

ARMS

***

"Okay," Jen whispered, holding her hands over Jamie's eyes, "Don't peak!"

She opened the front door to his house.

"Now!"

He looked around.

Pots, pans, a table, chairs,
leather, rugs, books, art,
poster bed,
        linens,
                toiletries. . .

It smells good in here—like lilacs? lilies? lasagna?

"Do you like it," Jen asked, walking herself back to the front door.

"It's. . .beautiful."

Her smiled reached ear-to-ear, "Thanks."

She turned to leave.

"Wait. . ."

"Yes?"

"Is that food I smell?"

"Just frozen lasagna in the oven."

"Have you eaten?"

**

CHEST/BACK

**

"May I speak with the Chair of the Department?"

"Dr. Rod's office hours are Monday, Wednesday and Friday from 1-2 in the afternoon."

"Fine, could you leave him a message? My name is Dr. Ted Kovich and it's urgent I speak with him. Thank you."

***

SHOULDER/ARM

***

"Ton Metal Laboratories."

"My name is Dr. Ted Kovich."

"Hello Dr. Kovich, how may we help you."

"I need to speak to your head metallurgical specialist."

"Dr. Con is out the office. May I take your name and number and have him call you as soon as possible?"

"It's rather urgent."

"I'll have him call as soon as possible. If it's urgent you can speak with Dr. Mitso."

"Fine."

"Please wait... ... ...Hello. Dr. Mitso speaking."

"Hello Dr. Mitso. My name is Dr. Kovich and I need . . ."

"Dr. Ted Kovich?"

"Yes. Do I know you?"

"You probably don't remember me but I was a graduate student working in your lab at BU."

"When?"

"Years ago! This is Asamu—Asamu Mitso."

"Oh…Asamu…"

"Yes, yes. It's me."

"…you don't know how glad I am to have found you!"

"Really?"

"Yes. I have a proposition for you."

***

LEGS

***

"So you really like the place?"

"It's just fine."

"The food's not so good. Sorry." Jen poked the cooling noodle.

"I don't usually eat this kind of stuff."

"Oh yeah. What do you eat?"

"Eggs. Meat. Complex carbs."

"Are you a bodybuilder?"

Jamie laughed, "Oh, I used to think about it every so often—when I was a kid. . ."

"You're not THAT old!"

How old am I now? That's right.

"Thanks. You?"

"Eighteen. . . and a half."

"Oh."

"Is that bad?"

"You're young."

Not too young

"Young can be fun," she kissed his cheek.

He pushed her back, hard.

"Listen, I don't know what you think is going on here but THIS this is

not."

"I'm sorry. . .I just didn't. . .oh God! I'd better go."

Jen grabbed her purse and rushed out the door. Jamie didn't

try to stop her. He just sat sifting between the memories of being

touched—of being wanted—of being loved and unloved and unwanted

and trying not to lose himself in the fury he felt sweeping over him

like wind through a flourmill.

CHEST/BACK

"Asamu!" Dr. Kovich exclaimed, spreading his arms to greet his former student with affection.

"Hello Dr. Kovich, it's great to see you again."

"I'm so glad you decided to come. How was your flight?"

"Good. I had to look Medford, Oregon up on the map though. It's a long way off from Texas."

"How long were you there for?"

"I got the job when I graduated BU with my PhD and moved there with my mom. . ."

"Well, enough chit-chat. We've got more work to do than is sane."

"So, room is included in my salary?"

"Yep, right back here," Ted pointed to the cot in the office and smiled.

Asamu's brow furrowed, "And my salary. . . it's what we agreed upon on the phone right?"

"Of course, don't you trust me?"

"I've been working in the chemistry biz too long to trust anyone."

Ted slapped Asamu's shoulder, "Then we'll get on just fine. By the way—your first job is to read ALL these binders."

Asamu looked at the shelves, "Anything good?"

"You'll tell me" Ted handed Asamu his first month's paycheck.

"Alright! It's your bucks," he replied, slapping the cashier's check against the palm of his hand.

RRRRRIIIIIIINNNNNNGGGGGGG

"Hello. Dr. Ted Kovich."

"Hello Dr. Kovich, my name is Dr. Rod. I have a message to return your call—'URGENT' it says."

"Yes! Dr. Rod! I'm so glad you called. Can I meet with you in person?"

"What is this regarding?"

"Believe me. It will be worth your time."

"Can you come to my office now?"

"I'll see you in ten."

"Five."

REST SHOULDER—CUFF HURTS WORK ARMSS

Jen had just walked into Whiting's Library when she

discovered a new face; "Who are you?"

"I'm Asamu. And you?"

"I'm Jen."

"Hi Jen. Are you a chemist too?"

"No no no I'm a personal assistant—I think."

Asamu squinched his face, "You mean you don't know?"

"Well, I am the last I knew but—it's. . .awkward."

Asamu patted the chair beside his cot/bed where he proceeded

to resume his former sprawling and {speed-reading}

[of ten] [journal] [binders at] [the same time—each] [opened]
 [with] [varying thickness] [between] [front/back] [covers].

"It's just that I really like Jamie and. . ."

"Jamie?"

"Yeah. . . you know—your boss!"

"Dr. Kovich is my boss."

"Well Dr. Kovich works for Jamie so 'technically' Jamie's your boss' boss."

"Never met him."

"Your loss."

"Hey, you hungry?" Asamu sat up straight.

He's a weird little guy and I don't know why but I kind of like him. He feels like—a friendly
                    {hummingbirdmoth butterf}y

"You buying?" Jen grinned.

"Sure, you know any good Thai places?"

"No but I know a great Lebanese joint down on the square."

"You got a car?"

"You buying the gas?"

"Woman after my own heart!"

"Don't get any ideas. . . so as I was saying," Jen continued while Asamu put the 10 binders atop his cot.

        In Jen's car:

". . . it's really awkward now because I kind-of came onto Jamie and he TOTALLY freaked out."

"No shit!"

"No shit."

"Didn't anyone ever tell you not to hit on your boss?"

"Yeah, you know I didn't really pay that good of attention in Career's Class."

***

CHEST/BACK/SHOULDER (easy)

***

"So what I need is at least one person, preferably two—more if you have them—that are VERY skilled in dissection."

"I see."

"It is critical that we begin immediately."

"I see."

"So. . .?"

Dr. Rod leaned back in his favorite leather chair. It had been worn to near-perfection over his ten-year-career—there.

"So what I hear you saying is that you have a corpse—an unpreserved corpse—that you want my assistance to dissect either personally or via my students. Is this correct?"

"Exactly."

"By chance, Dr. Kovich, are you aware that you must register all corpses with the Health department immediately and that there are strict guidelines as to how a body is to be maintained if no preservatives are used."

That son-of-a-bitch is treating me like a neophyte! Who the FUCK does he think he IS? Settle down! You NEED his help. Seal THIS DEAL!

"Yes, sir."

"Is the body registered with the Health Department?"

"Yes."

"Has it been inspected?"

"Yes."

"Do you have the signed documentation?"

"Yes, here in my briefcase."

Dr. Rod leaned forward, looked at the papers Dr. Kovich pushed across his desk and sighed like he was carrying weight greater than an Atlas Stone, "Very well. I charge by the hour."

***

ARMS (easy—shoulder buggered)/LEGS

***

Jamie read, again, "I don't know how to tell you so I'll just tell you. When Gene died. . ."

If I never hear that fucking name again it will be too soon. Why, Annie, why couldn't you love ME like that?

". . .part of me went into the ground. The part of me you always felt hidden from you. Well, it wasn't—it was dead; death was trapped in my living body because I swore Gene's death would not be in vain.

I never wanted anyone else left paralyzed from the soul-out, so I. . ."

You mean like you've left me?

". . .tried to play it fair—at first. I did what the 'experts' said. I learned. I educated myself. And then I started asking questions—but no one had any answers to help Gene—to save him. I learned about hexavalent chromium and I started studying it as deeply as my brain could but you know me, Jamie, I'm no brain. That was what I loved most about you—I could be me, just me and I knew you loved me even though I was a failure.

Anyway, I wrote hundreds of letters to scientists and researchers—thousands maybe—but no one would help. So I dug deeper. There's a saying, "The more you stir the more stink." With Cr6 nothing could be truer.

I found that there were some pretty logical reasons why no one had answers. You can read about it all in my journals at the library; the point of this diary—this journal—is to finally give you what you always asked of me but I couldn't give.

I hope you will come to understand how important my work was and that it was its importance and not my lack of caring for you that kept me silent all those years. Love Anne"

The alarm chittered. 4:30 a.m.

Time to work out

"Hey Bill."

"Hey Jamie, how's it goin'?"

"Can I ask you something;?"

"Shoot."

"Will you tell me about Anne?"

"Ahhh, kid. . . why you wanna' go diggin' up the dead?"

"Because I need to know."

"She was your wife," he laughed, "you probably knew all you needed to know—if you know what I mean."

"Sometimes wives lie."

"Annie? No, Man, I tell you. She was a straight shooter if I ever knew one. I loved that kid, so watch what you say."

"I loved her too but you know we met after Gene died—and she kept a lot inside."

Bill rubbed the back of his neck, "I know THAT."

"Why do you say THAT?"

"Well, it's just that she'd been trainin' in my gym since she was but a kid and then all of a sudden Gene gets sick and I NEVER see her again. I mean she just quit workin' out, quit seein' her friends, it was like she was dyin' too."

"That's right. That's what she wrote."

"Wrote?"

"Her letters to me."

"Well, then. There's your answers."

"I'd just like to know what she was like—you know—before Gene got sick."

Bill dropped his head down a bit so that he had to look through his thick, wiry eyebrows to see Jamie's eyes, "Listen, Son. You fell in love with her after—she fell in love with you after. What was before, well that doesn't concern you does it? And I'll tell you one thing: the dead are dead for a reason—to remind us livin' that we still are—and it's time to start liftin'! Got it?"

"Got it—hey Bill?"

"Yeah?"

"That was 2."

"Wise Ass."

***

SHOULDER (cortisone feels good now)

***

"Hello Dr. Rod," Jen beamed to the man coming into the Gene Whiting Library.

"Hello. You are?"

"Jen Stell. I'm taking your Intro to Biology for non-science majors next quarter."

I HATE that class. Son-of-a-bitch provost and her 'make-overs' for education. 20 years! 20 years since I got my PhD! I shouldn't have to be teaching crap like that

"Oh. . .that's. . .nice. Is Dr. Kovich here?"

"Yes. In back."

Jen pointed then whispered, "The cold storage room, if you know what I mean."

Lovely

"Thank you."

"Oh, you're welcome Dr. Rod."

Nice smile

    Dr. Rod entered the frigid room where the body of Anne Whiting rested. Primary incisions had already been made through the skull plates. The large bone end plates had been removed from both femurs as well as fingernails and skin/tissue as well as samples of hair from the head, the arm, the pubis and lip.

Dr. Kovich had sent samples of Anne Whiting's bone, hair, skin, nail to vastly different specialty laboratories. The results were beginning to come in and Dr. Kovich was particularly excited on the day that happened to be Dr. Rod's first day of their epic.

"Ah, Dr. Rod, so glad you could make it," Dr. Kovich was peeling the epithelial layer from Anne's nipple.

"Your check cleared."

Ted laughed, "Well you'd better be worth it."

"Oh, believe me, I am."

Dr. Rod had dreamed of being a neurosurgeon ever since he could remember dreaming. Unfortunately, he was to find out—during his first year at Stanford and while volunteering at a hospital—that he fainted at the sight of blood. Rethinking his life-plan he set a course upon neurochemistry only to find his artful hands lent themselves most strongly to biology.

"It is vital we have clean samples of the striatum."

"But of course. Do you have the chemicals I asked for?" Dr, Rod sneered.

"Yes."

"The tools, the equipment?" Dr. Rod asked without really listening as he was already surveying the cranial incisions.

"Yes."

"Who the hell made these cuts?"

"Why? Is something wrong?"

Dr. Rod looked up from Anne's splitting head, "No. . .they're wonderful."

Ted smiled, "Asamu will be happy to hear it."

"Who?"

Asamu suddenly burst in, carrying three notebooks, each opened and resting on each other, "Dr. Kovich. . ."

"Asamu, get those things out of here!"

"Oh, sorry. Sorry. But I MUST speak with you!"

Dr. Rod had begun his delicate work but looked up, "Should I hear this?"

Asamu looked at Ted, who looked at the binders and answered before his young friend could, "I seriously doubt it."

Dr. Rod nodded and got back to his work.

Before Asamu could set the binders down to show Ted what he'd learned, Jamie walked in the front door. Both Ted and Asamu looked at Jen, who suddenly looked as if she'd grown a good ten degrees hotter particularly about the face.

"Hello," Jamie said without looking at Jen.

"Jamie," Ted left Asamu mouthing the same words coming from his own mouth: "I must speak with you."/ "I must speak with you."

"Fine," Jamie said to Ted, "Let's get some air."

Ted left with Jamie.

Asamu stormed off to his office/bedroom.

Jen watched the clock tick until 5 p.m. without a single phone-ring or thing to do and left.

Dr. Rod worked until nearly midnight excavating the deepest recess of Anne Whiting's brain.

***

LEGS

***

"I didn't know you liked Lebanese food," Jamie said to Ted.

"Asamu said it was good. Listen. We have to talk about money."

"Okay, talk."

"Can I take your order?"

I don't know 'can' you? I hate the way our language is going

"I'd like special number one please," Ted replied.

Jamie nodded, "Me as well."

Let it go Ted let it go

Server: anything to drink?

Jamie: water

Ted: Vodka

"Very good. I'll be right back with your drinks."

"I didn't take you for a drinker Doc."

"Ted, remember."

"Ah yes. Drinker Ted."

"Funny. Now, this is serious. I don't know how much you know about science and research but what you're telling me to do, what Anne's journals are asking us. . ."

"Us? That's right. You needed help. Who'd you get?"

"It doesn't matter—to you I'm sure—the point is. . ."

"It DOES matter! Can they be trusted?"

"With what?"

Jamie leaned across the table such that his nose was a straw-length's from Ted's, "With Anne."

Ted raised his eyebrows, "Uh. . .I don't exactly know what you mean but if you're asking whether Asamu and Dr. Rod are ethical, I personally know Asamu and Dr. Rod was—at one time—one of the Nation's top neurobiologists."

"Was?"

"Yeah, well, academia is a bitch alright. Let's just leave it at that. Anyway, we're getting WAY off point."

"Money."

"Yes!"

Ted opened a file he'd carefully prepared and pushed it towards Jamie:

"Okay," Jamie said looking at the 20-font-sized $ value.

"Okay? You sure? That's a HELL-of-a-lot of money!"

Jamie let out a sigh. The one thing Anne had asked of him was that he manage the library and to make sure that the research on the relationship between hexavalent chromium exposure and parkinsonism succeeded.

Anne had left her money, Gene's money, to him: she left him her life insurance policy and he had sold the house in New Zealand.

Still, the dollar figure in front of him meant that nearly two-thirds of everything he had would be exacted.

"I said okay. But," he looked very seriously at Ted, "don't spend more than this."

Ted's eyes flittered when he said he wouldn't. In all the years of working security Jamie had learned that flittery eyes meant lies.

But hers were cool as ponds, still as canes on trees—and she lied

"Here you go: one water one vodka."

"Cheers."

"To what," Ted asked.

"To answers."

"Amen."

"You a religious man Doc?"

"I wish you'd call me Ted. And, as a matter-of-fact. . . I really don't know."

Jamie shook his head, "You're so weird."

***

LEGS

***

His alarm had just gone off. He was pulling himself out of bed, cringing because his thighs were still sore from squats the day before, when he heard a knock on his door.

■■■

Who the hell would be knocking at 4:00 in the morning?

Each

    step

        down

            the

                stairs

                    made him suck in air,

like the hundreds of pounds that had been on his back were still there.

He flipped on the porch light. It was Jen and she looked like shit.

"Jen, what are you doing here?"

Mascara streaked lines beneath her eyelashes and she wreaked

of stale beer.

"I juusss had to tell you that I'm not someone you can juuusss

disssmisss like a ssschoolgurll."

She tottered and suddenlyvomited onto the deck.

■ ■

Retching (wretching) over and again. Heaving drink of

nothing her body had needed—an ancient mariner—an albatross;

Jamie lifted her up, gagging himself in the process.

"Come on," he said—softly. He'd been there before.

"Dooonnnn tutch me!"

"Come on, Jen, it's okay. Let's get you cleaned up."

Then she broke and he watched her tender eyelashes rain ink down her {almost-womanly} cheeks; down his chest where her sticky sweat-matted hair rested and she trembled as she told him everything she felt, everything she thought and wanted and dreamed—everything he'd wanted to hear for years—spewed from her stinking little mouth and he pulled her close to him and cried for the first time since Anne's death because he was holding on…and she was living.

***

RRRIIINNNGGG RRRIIIINNNGGG RRRIIINNNGG
RRRIIINNNGG

Come on Bill. . . pick up

RRRIIINNNGG RRRIIINNGGG RRRINNNGGG
RRRIINNGGIIIRNNNGNII
I know you're there.

RRRIIINNG

"Yeah."

"Bill it's Jamie."

"Where the hell are ya?"

"Hey I can't come today."

"Yeah, I've heard that one before."

"I know. A friend's in trouble."

"What kind of trouble?"

"The dumb-young kind."

"Skunk-Drunk!"

"Yep. I'll see ya later."

"Your loss. We gotta killer arm one today, Rocko's idea."

"Figures!"

***

"Listen, I sent those samples Dr. Rod prepared to the labs in California, Texas, Florida and Minnesota like you asked but I REALLY need to talk to you."

"Okay Asamu, what is it?"

"You need to read these."

"Please tell me it's not more of the same. . ."

"Look at the name!"

Dear Dr. Ted Kovich, my name is Anne Whiting and I'm researching the biological effects of hexavalent chromium. I am contacting you because your work on chromium was published in Molecular. . .

"Son-of-a-bitch!"

"And you replied, look—she kept your letter—here."

Dear Ms. Whiting

Both CrVI and CrIII can be detected in human tissues, however, CrVI is short-lived in human blood or tissues unless there has been a massive intake via industrial accident or suicide attempt. . .

"Ted, did you know how Anne Whiting died?"

"Chromium poisoning."

"Yes, but did you read the last 20 binders of Personal Observations?"

"No. That was your job."

"She progressively increased her hexavalent chromium intake. . ."

"I know that, ingestion, topical, inhalation, intramuscular injection and intravenous injection."

"But that was not what killed her."

"Okay, then what."

"Her last binder shows her close observations as to her body's functioning, physically and cognitively, and close comparison between test results but look here. . ."

Dr. Kovich looked down at the scribbling. It looked like it had been done in the hand of a two-year-old. The letters were hardly decipherable:

"There is only one way to know the extent to which hexavalent chromium can damage the body—a doctor once told me but I've since forgotten his name—this will, I suspect, be my final entry. . ."

And with very small numbers and letters such that Asamu gave Dr. Ted a magnifying glass, it read:

250 cc iv sodium dichromate/saline 80/20

"That's not possible!" Ted set the glass down, "She couldn't have done that. . . that much. . . it's not,"

Jamie!

Dr. Kovich ran to the phone:

RRRIIIIIIIIIIIINNNNNNNNNGGGGGGGGGGGGGGG
RRRRRRRRRRIIIIIIIIIIIIIIIIIIIINNNNNNNNNNNNNGGGGGGG
RRRRRRRRRRRRRRRIIIIIIIIIIIIIIIIIIIINNNNNNNNNNNNNNNNG

Come on, come on, pick up the damned phone damn it!

RRRRRRRRRRRRIIIIIIIIINNNNNNNNNGGGGGGGGGGGGGG
RRRRRRRRRRRRRRRIIIIIIIIINNNNNNNNNGGGGGGGGGGGGGG
RRRRRRRRRRRRRIIIIIIIIIIINNNNNNNNNNNNNGGGGGGGGGG

SHIT!

"Listen. I'm going over there you stay here and whatever you do DON'T tell Dr. Rod any of this when he comes in got it!"

"Yes, but I don't really understand what the big deal is?"

"Don't understand! I don't have time. Just do what I say. When Dr. Rod comes in have him work like everything is just the way it was."

"Isn't it. . ."

Ted was already out the door and scrambling into his car.

Son-of-a-bitch! Why didn't he TELL me she o.d.ed. Fuck! This totally fucks up the samples! SHIT! What the hell am I going to do now! Damn it. I knew I shouldn't have gotten involved in this project. Why does this shit ALWAYS happen to me. Fucking red light! Look at them—those damn students, so fucking happy. They just don't know… just wait—YOU DUMBSHITS! You'll get yours someday, when you grow up. Son-of-a-bitch, what the fuck am I going to do???? Okay, okay, think, think, okay, we have the PET scans, MRIs, SHIT, fucking novices, just my FUCKING LUCK she'd fuck this up! That BITCH— hold on, that's a bit over the top—okay, we have. . . we have. . .SHIT we have SHIT IS WHAT WE HAVE. FUCK, all those tissue samples and they're fucking worthless. It's a fucking poisoning versus chronic exposure. SHIT.
Okay, settle down. Settle down. Yeah, that's right, remember, Jamie— he's the big dumb protective guy, the guy who could kick your ass in two seconds guy, okay, FUCK I'm SO PISSED! SHIT. Okay. Settle down. Here's the house. Breathe. Breathe. Ask don't tell. Ask don't accuse. FUCK FUCK FUCK! Okay. It's out of my system. Okay. Here we go. .

BING BONG

Ask don't tell ask don't tell ask don't tell WHERE the fuck is he?? Settle down. It is only 8 in the morning, maybe he's still sleeping. Lucky son-of-a bitch. Settle down, breathe

BING BONG BING BONG

The door opened to Jamie standing in his shorts. It was the first time Ted had seen him without his shirt on.

"Uhh…uh…"

"Yeah Doc, what is it?"

Shit, yeah. That's right, uh, okay, ask don't what? What was it, shit

"Uh, Doc. . . Ted?"

"Yeah, yeah, Jamie. DAMN IT why didn't you tell me!" Ted screamed.

Did I just say that? Please tell me I only thought that

"What the fuck!"

Shit! I did say it

"I mean," Ted recoiled, taking a step backward, "did you find Anne with the syringe."

Jamie took a step towards Ted like he was going to grab his throat but Ted suddenly found himself trying to support, what he swore must have been two tons of flesh.

A few minutes later Jamie opened his eyes to find Ted propping him up against his wide-opened front door.

"Wha. . .what happened."

Ted laughed, "You fainted."

"Yeah right."

"No seriously," Ted started full-belly laughing, "I mean like big-time!"

"Shut up." Jamie tried to stand but his legs were still sore and seemed wobbly. "Did I really?"

"Yep, flat as a pancake," Ted grinned, beamed really.

"Shit," he said, rubbing his head, "you want some coffee?"

"Sure."

Once inside Ted looked around. It had been the first time he'd been to Jamie's house. He whistled through his front teeth, "Nice place."

"It's a rental."

"So's mine but it's NOTHING like this."

Jamie poured a cup of coffee from the pot that had been

—sitting full—on its burner four hours.

"What brings you here Doc."

"You didn't tell me Anne was a suicide."

"You didn't ask."

"Well it was KIND OF IMPORTANT!"

"Why?"

Ted sipped his coffee

BLAGHHH This is the worst coffee I've ever had

He lifted his cup, "Good cuppa'"

Jamie smiled, "I haven't heard that term since I lived in New

Zealand."

"Yeah, well, the chit-chat and all. The thing is we're really FUCKED

now!"

Ted slammed the cup down.

Jamie leaned against the counter, "What can we do?"

Ted hung his head, "I don't know. . . I really don't know."

"Can you figure it out?"

"You don't understand."

"Listen, Ted, I understand one thing. Anne believed you were the one to bust this thing wide open. I know she could have given—herself—to other people but she picked you. You wanna know why?"

"Sure."

"Because you've gotten fucked over so many times you know what it feels like. The day before she died she. . ."

Jamie stared at the counter tiles,

". . . told me about a scientist she admired because every time he got close to the truth the politicians and businessmen. . ."

Jamie laughed under his breath, ". . .she called them identical twins, anyway," he continued, "they'd pull this guy's funding every time he got just within reach. Sound like anyone you know Doc?"

Ted didn't look up.

"She figured she'd give you the shot you'd never have gotten legit."

Ted stared into the blackness of his cup, "The problem is . . . now her body isn't a chronic, progressive exposure. Her body—now—as it sits, is a poisoning. It makes a big difference and I just don't know. . ."

"Well, I know—you'll figure something out."

Just then Jen came staggering down the stairs wearing one of Jamie's T-shirts and rubbing her eyes.

Ted looked back-and-forth between the two of them

Typical! No wonder Charles Atlas made millions!

"I'd better go."

"Think about what I said Doc."

"I will. Hey, don't say anything to Dr. Rod. . . not yet."

"Don't worry. I haven't said but a couple words to that guy—I don't like *him*."

"Is that coffee?" Jen asked.

Jamie dumped the pot in the sink, "Let me make you some fresh stuff."

Dr. Ted took the hint and split.

"Don't go to any bother on my part."

"It's no bother," Jamie smiled, "you sure your stomach can handle it?"

Jen rested her hand on her belly, "I hope so."

Jamie scooped coffee grounds into the basked, "So. . . you hit it pretty hard last night."

"Yeah."

He poured water into the machine, "That your normal?"

"No. Never again!"

"How'd you get it anyway?"

"NOW you sound old."

"I guess so. Cream/sugar?"

"Yes please."

Jamie handed her the mug she'd specially picked out for him—it had an iridescent-looking dragonfly resting on a pile of freshly-threshed hay. She took a sip.

Ummm good coffee

"Thanks," she said, looking at the tan liquid, "for taking care of me."

"Ditto."

"Huh?"

"Nothing. Hungry?"

"NO!"

Jamie laughed.

"That's not EVEN funny!"

He handed her a couple of aspirin and a tall glass of cold water,

"Sure-fire hangover remedy."

"Speaking from experience?"

"I wasn't always old you know."

"You're still not. . .are you?"

"27."

"18 ½"

"I know. You told me—before."

"Hey, I'm really sorry about dumping like that…and then the whole
kiss thing."

"No. I'm sorry. I just can't seem to let myself feel…anything."

"I wish I had THAT problem!"

He touched her cheek, "No you don't. You really don't," and leaned
over the counter to kiss her little mouth but she pulled away, "No,
don't! I have YUCK-mouth!" Just then she grabbed his hand and led
him to the bathroom.

"What say we get cleaned up," she said, smiling as she dropped his shirt onto the tile floor and climbed into the showerheads whose water had already begun to steam the mirrors of a house preparing itself for winter.

***

ARMS

***

Okay, think, Ted, think. First, no more tissue samples. That's good. Saves a lot of money, but wait, maybe we should do tissue samples because. . . I wish I knew. Comparative PETs with documented dosages—I can get that published. It is interesting the different routes of exposure and predictable depletion of dopamine neurons via PET: that's publishable. MRI, again, lesioning with dosages, publishable. DAMN! I wish her current state was due to chronic. It's so fucking impressive! The CrIII is present with immuno-proteins within the striatum's Lewy bodies. It's not Cr6 and I knew it wouldn't be but it is just what I'd proposed years ago—that it's an activated form of CrIII-bound-protein that causes an immune response and it is THAT IMMUNE RESPONSE that kills the neurons and causes lesioning but SHIT, I can't use her brain tissues. It would have been the breakthrough of the century!

Then he saw it. He'd nearly forgotten all about the black leather journal.

What the hell—there's nothing to lose. . .

206

He took a pair of scissors and cut the leather strap from the heart-lock.

LET HIM **KISS** ME WITH THE **KISSES** OF HIS **MOUTH**: FOR THY LOVE IS BETTER THAN WINE.

DRAW ME, WE WILL RUN AFTER THEE:
THE KING HATH BROUGHT ME INTO HIS **CHAMBERS**:
WE WILL BE GLAD AND REJOICE IN THEE,
WE WILL REMEMBER THY LOVE MORE THAN WINE:
THE UPRIGHT LOVE THEE.

TELL ME, O THOU WHOM MY SOUL LOVETH,
WHERE THOU FEEDEST,
WHERE THOU MAKEST THEY FLOCK TO REST AT NOON:
FOR WHY SHOULD I BE AS ONE THAT TURNETH ASIDE BY THE FLOCKS OF THY COMPANIONS?
I HAVE COMPARED THEE, O MY LOVE, TO A COMPANY OF **HORSES** IN PHARAOH'S CHARIOTS.

THY **CHEEKS** ARE COMELY WITH ROWS OF JEWELS,
THY **NECK** WITH CHAINS OF GOLD.

A BUNDLE OF MYRRH IS MY WELL-BELOVED UNTO ME;
HE SHALL LIE ALL NIGHT BETWIXT MY BREASTS.

BEHOLD, THOU ART FAIR, MY LOVE;
BEHOLD, THOU ART FAIR;
THOU HAST **DOVES' EYES.**

BEHOLD, THOU ART FAIR, MY BELOVED,
YEA PLEASANT:
ALSO **OUR BED** IS GREEN.

I AM THE ROSE OF SHARON AND THE **LILY** OF THE VALLEYS.

I SAT UNDER HIS SHADOW WITH GREAT DELIGHT AND HIS FRUIT WAS
SWEET TO MY TASTE.

MY BELOVED SPAKE, AND SAID UNTO ME,
RISE UP, MY LOVE, MY FAIR ONE,
AND COME AWAY.

BY NIGHT ON MY BED I SOUGHT HIM WHOM MY SOUL LOVETH:
I SOUGHT HIM, BUT FOUND HIM NOT.

MY BELOVED IS GONE DOWN INTO HIS GARDEN,
TO THE BEDS OF SPICES,
TO FEED IN THE GARDENS,
AND TO GATHER LILIES.
HOW BEAUTIFUL ARE THY FEET WITH SHOES, O PRINCE'S DAUGHTER!
THE JOINTS OF THY THIGHS ARE LIKE JEWELS,
THE WORK OF THE HANDS OF A CUNNING WORKMAN.

THY NAVAL IS LIKE A ROUND GOBLET,
WHICH WANTETH NOT LIQUOR:
THY BELLY IS LIKE A HEAP OF WHEAT SET ABOUT WITH LILIES.
THY TWO BREASTS ARE LIKE TWO YOUNG ROES THAT ARE TWINS.
THY NECK IS AS A TOWER OF IVORY;
THINE EYES LIKE THE FISHPOOLS IN HESHBON, BY THE GATE OF
BATHRABBIM:
THY NOSE IS AS A TOWER OF LEBANON WHICH LOOKETH TOWARD
DAMASCUS.
THINE HEAD UPON THEE IS LIKE CARMEL,
AND THE HAIR OF THINE HEAD LIKE PURPLE;
THE KING IS HELD IN THE GALLERIES.
HOW FAIR AND PLEASANT ART THOU, O LOVE, FOR DELIGHTS!
THIS THY STATURE IS LIKE TO A PALM TREE,
AND THY BREASTS TO CLUSTERS OF GRAPES.

I SAID, I WILL GO UP TO THE PALM TREE,
I WILL TAKE HOLD OF THE BOUGHS THEREOF:
NOW ALSO THY BREASTS SHALL BE AS CLUSTERS OF THE VINE,
AND THE SMELL OF THY NOSE LIKE APPLES;
AND THE ROOF OF THY MOUTH LIKE THE BEST WINE FOR MY
BELOVED,

THAT GOETH DOWN SWEETLY,
CAUSING THE LIPS OF THOSE THAT ARE ASLEEP TO SPEAK.

I AM MY BELOVED'S, AND HIS **DESIRE** IS TOWARD ME.

WOW! What the heck was that! That was totally HOT! Dang. Anne Whiting, wheeeew!

The next day Asamu found Ted photocopying part of a black leather journal. He handed the sheets to Asamu, keeping the journal by his side.

"What's this," Asamu asked.

"You tell me."

Asamu started reading and stopped, "Uh, is this part of my job description?"

"Yes. Have you ever heard this before?"

"Not sure, maybe. Shakespeare? Donne? Something literary?"

"Find out and tell me ASAP."

"OKEE DOKEE BOSS!"

Why do I always get the shit jobs

Asamu was storming out the front door just as Jen was coming in.

"What's wrong?"

Asamu held up his photocopies.

"What is it?"

"I don't know. I'm TOLD to find out."

"Let me take a look."

Jen looked at the words. The delicate handwriting.

"It's a woman's."

"Good guess. Anything else Sherlock?"

"Yeah, it's from the Bible."

"No SHIT!"

"Yeah, it's from Song of Solomon."

"How do you know."

"Because I read the Bible."

"Uh oh."

"Is that bad?"

"Uh I think I have to say 'no' because I can get into trouble if I say anything else."

"Okay, so you're off the hook. Why isn't it good?"

"Let me just say that my experiences with "" Christians has been not-very-good."

"How do you know I'm not Jewish?"

"Just a guess."

"You're racist!"

"Funny! Hungry?"

"Sure. Same place?"

"Number One Special."

Walking out to the car Asamu looked at Jen, "I didn't know the Bible was so, uh…"

"Graphic?"

"Hot."

"WELL, let me TELL ya'!"

***

REST

***

"Hello Dr. Kovich, can I help you?"

"I'd like to see Dr. Rod."

"He's with a student just now. Have a seat. It shouldn't be much longer."

He opened the black leather journal:

"What have I to say worth saying? I am nothing. This life—nothing. If not for what I knew I needed to do, I should have been buried in the ground with Gene. Will anyone ever know a love such as that which burns, which aches in me every moment—dreaming. . .awake? Can I be forgiven? Dear Lord?"

For what?

"He can see you now."

A young girl all smiles and soft nearly-babyfat-skin walked out of Dr. Rod's office.

Lucky son-of-a-bitch

Dr. Rod smiled, "Come in, Dr. Kovich, come in," as he sat in his leather chair, "what can I do for you?"

"Your student?"

"Perqs of teaching in a small school. What brings you here?"

Dr. Kovich put Anne's black leather journal inside his briefcase, then extracted a singular paper which he handed over. Dr. Rod read—Ted watched his eyes.

A speedreader. Lucky SOB in THAT too!

Dr. Rod handed the paper back to Ted, "I see," he said.

Ted sighed, "So you see...there's really nothing more I can do."

Dr. Rod replied, dryly, "Dr. Kovich, that would seem quite true of you."

"So. . . I won't be needing your services further."

Dr. Rod's eyes looked as piercing as a badger's, "I fear, dear Dr. Kovich, you've overlooked a small matter."

"And that would be?"

"Toxicity is dose-dependant. . ."

"Listen Dr. Rod, I've had just about enough of your. . ."

". . .and it really doesn't mean a damn thing that she o.d.'d because she'd already established a systematically progressive baseline for exposure and—in fact, if you were thinking outside your toxicological mind you'd just about be having a party at this point!"

Ted said nothing.

"She gave you everything. The full spectrum. . ."

Still.

Nothing.

"Did you not read my reports on the basal ganglia tissue samples?"

"Of course!"

"Then you know, categorically the cells were classified into stage III parkinsonism of unknown etiology."

"Yes, but she killed herself—she poisoned herself with Cr6."

"Yes, but the PET scans show she was already stage III prior to the act."

"I know I know but I don't know where you're going with this. The opposition will tear us apart when they find out it was a poisoning let alone SUICIDE!"

Dr. Rod sucked in air and looked at the ceiling.

Why, Lord? Why am I surrounded by these people with so little vision. Anne had vision. Kudos to you Anne! Wherever you are.

"Dr. Kovich, let's try this again. . ."

***

CHEST

***

"So you and Jamie huh?"

"I don't kiss and tell."

"Like hell you don't."

"Seriously. He was a perfect gentleman and, whether or not you believe me or not, I'm not that kind of girl."

Asamu rolled his eyes.

"Really," Jen protested.

"So you're telling me you're drunk, crying, PUKING and he's taking care of you. You wake up in HIS shirt and NOTHING else and NOTHING happened?"

"I didn't say 'nothing' I just said I'm not that kind of girl," Jen grinned.

"Okay little-miss-politician-want-to-be!"

"Here you go: 2 #1s."

"Thanks."

"I just love the food here," Jen said, stuffing the sweet, earthy taste into her mouth.

"Me too. I'm so glad we found it."

"We?"

"Oh yeah. You—you seem to find a lot of things!!!"

"Ha ha. But seriously. . ."

"Uh oh. I never like sentences that start with 'but seriously'."

". . .I really care for him."

"Oh yeah. Heard that a million times. Great-looking guy, all muscles and tons of money, sure the cute girl 'really cares for him' but would you if he was dead broke?"

"Yes," Jen said, putting her fork down and staring Asamu dead in the eye, "I would. There is something I feel when I'm with him that I've never felt before."

Asamu huffed, "And you're HOW old?"

"Oh shut up!"

"I rest my case."

***

BACK W/: Rocko, Steve, Max, Ty, Jerry & Bill:

"You look like shit Jamie!"

"Thanks Rocko. I heard you guys hit arms hard."

"Yeah, leave it to me," Rocko grinned.

"He likes to toot his own horn," Bill laughed.

"Yeah, wait 'till Leg-Day," Max piped in, "Jamie'll bury YOU Rocko!"

"Oh yeah, check out these," Rocko flopped his quads back and forth.

Steve chimed, "If you guys are done being total assholes you want to train or what?"

Ty jumped up into Dead position.

"Leave it to Ty—the all-business-guy," Jamie piped.

"Yeah, I'd like to train sometime this century myself," Jerry chirped.

"Okay. . ." Bill interrupted, "if everyone's ready may we start?"

"Hey Bill," called out the chorus, "why you bein' so nice today?"

"It's my birthday."

"No shit?"

"Yep, 80."

"No fuckin' way!" Rocko yelled, "I never knew you were THAT old!"

"Old enough to know an ugly mug when I see one!"

"Ouch," Jerry, Max and Ty managed to sting in unison, "There's the guy we've grown to love."

Jamie was quiet. He wanted to lose his thoughts

ANNE, JEN, HIM, CHROMIUM, MONEY

in pain, sweat and the smell of rusting iron but he whispered to Bill after the weights had been set, "Happy birthday."

"Thanks. You okay?"

"I don't know."

"Well, that's a good sign."

"Yeah?"

"Yeah. It's when you DON'T know you're fucked up that you got a real problem."

The guys all nodded.

"Girl?" Rocko asked.

Ty slapped him, "As if you have to ask! It's always a girl makes a guy look like THAT!"

Jamie nodded.

Max sat next to him on the bench, waiting his turn to take his set, "Good or bad?"

"Both."

"Yep. . . women. Not like weights. Not cold to touch but 'ouch' ice-queens every one of 'em."

"You just pick bad ones," Bill laughed, "besides, stop yammerin! It's your set."

Bill sat next to Jamie, "Do I know her?"

Jamie looked him in the eye, "Probably not."

I hope she gets you over Annie

"It's your set," Bill said.

Jamie bent over the bar. Back straight, triceps tight, neck muscles flexed and ribcage moving in and out before he took a deep breath and

Deadlift clang deadlift clang deadlift clang deadlift clang deadlift clang deadlift clang deadlift clang

Rocko yelled, "You got it Jamie! Keep goin'"
"Yeah, two more—PULL it!" Ty's voice always boomed—like a gun.

Jamie breathed out and in

Deadlift clang   deadlift

he held the weight just a moment. Everything was quiet except the slight sound of the weightplates trembling fatigue

CLANG!

Goodbye Annie

Later. . .

Jamie unlocked the door to the Gene Whiting Library for the Advancement of Chromium Studies.

It was dark but the seasons had changed; it was the middle of winter and first thing in the morning. Still.

Jamie didn't turn on the lights. He knew everything by heart in the dark and he wanted to be alone with Annie.

Inside the cold he pulled her sheet back. It was the first time, since she'd died, he saw her...

My God, Annie! They've carved you to bits! It doesn't even look like you anymore. I'm sorry
...he kissed her skinned lips...

I don't want to die

and he re-covered her peeled-back eyelids.

***

SHOULDER DAY

***

RRRRRRIIIIIIIIIIIINNNNNNNNNNNNNNNNNGGGGGGGGGGGG

"Hello."

"Ted?"

"Yeah. Jamie?"

"Yeah. Can I come over?"

"To MY place?"

"Yeah."

"Uh. . .I guess so. It's nothing special."

"I don't care about that. . . I just need to talk. . ."

"Okay. You know where I live?"

"No, not really."

"You go down by the supermarket, take a right, go over the railroad
tracks and make a quick left. . ."

***

LEG DAY

***

"So what are you going to do now?"

"I don't know. I guess wait and see."

"Do you think he feels the same way about you?"

"I do. I can't really explain it. It's like I knew the moment I looked
into his eyes that I would be with him for the rest of my life."

Asamu got real close to Jen, "And you guys didn't. . ."

"Nope. We hugged, kissed, touched, cried, talked, cried, etcetera . . . it really wasn't about sex."

"Really?"

"It was deeper, somehow, stronger."

"Are you attracted to him?"

"GOD yes!"

"Him to you?"

"It's funny you ask that. When I first met him I thought he was gay."

"Uh oh! You know what they say about bodybuilder guys."

"I hadn't really thought about that. It was just that he didn't look at me like a piece of meat—like every other guy does."

"I resemble that comment!"

"Yes you do! I certainly knew YOU liked me."

"That obvious?"

"Let's just say I appreciated your 'forthrightness.' But with Jamie it was like he didn't notice me at all in that way but when we were finally together there was no question in my mind that he was attracted. . ."

"Say no more, PLEASE! I'll take the check. Lunch is on me—I haven't heard something that good since I left Texas."

"Do you miss it?"

"I miss my mom."

"Girlfriend?"

"Girls don't like science-geeks. At least that's been my experience."

"You should meet my roommate. She's into genetics."

"No shit?"

"No shit."

"Girl, why didn't you say something before?"

"I had to make sure you were an okay guy because she's really nice. Christian too." Jen smiled, "That won't be a problem will it?"

"You've shown me the err of my ways. There is at least ONE good Christian that I know."

"Hopefully you'll be able to say you know a lot more soon."

***

"What's going on," Ted asked as Jamie walked in and looked around for something to sit on, finding only a folding chair next to a card table covered with scribbled notes and a black leather journal.

Ted pointed to the chair. Jamie sat down.

"Would you like some coffee."

"Sure."

"How do you take it?"

"Black, thanks. Listen Doc. . ."

Ted

"Yes?"

"I'm getting out."

Ted was filling his Mr. Coffee pot with tap water, "What do you mean
by that?"

"I mean I'm going to leave you the library, the stuff, and
1half/2mi'money."

"And the other half?"

"The other half is what Annie left to me. . . to do what I really wanted
to do with it. . ."

"And?"

Ted poured the water into the maker's reservoir

". . .and I. . .something has happened. . ."

"Jen?"

"Yes. . . how did you know?"

"I'm a scientist. I'm not blind."

Jamie smiled, "Well it's just that I feel something for her. . .I don't really understand. . ."

"Those are the best kinds of feelings. Believe me!"

"You really think so?"

"Yes and I think. . ."

The coffee pot sputtered and sizzled

". . .Anne would want you to. . ."

"How would you know what Annie would want?"

Ted looked at Jamie. He wanted to tell him what he'd learned. He wanted his friend to be free from the ghost of Anne Whiting because he knew, definitively, that Anne Whiting had never loved ANYONE except Gene Whiting.

". . .it's just a guess. But I know that if I really loved someone I'd want them to have love in their life—if that's what God wanted for them…"

"I thought you didn't believe in God."

"Even scientists can learn."

"Thanks Doc. . . I mean Ted."

"It's alright. I'm getting used to Doc—from you."

Jamie stood up, "You're alright. Will you keep in touch?"

"You really want me to?"

"Yeah, but no more chemistry okay. A 'I met a girl and we're having fun' is good but if I never hear about hexavalent chromium again it would suit me just fine."

"I know the feeling—sometimes."

As Jamie got into his car Ted leaned his head close, "And Anne? Do you want to know what happens to Anne?"

"I know what happened to Anne. She died. You got her body, that's the end."

Ted nodded his head...

Good

...went back inside.

He didn't have any coffee. Ah well I might as well

...and poured himself a cup.

He opened up the final page of Anne's black leather journal and re-read:

Dear Diary,

This will be my last entry into you. I am putting you into your own library. Someday, someone will come for you and you will be able to tell them who I am. How I've loved. When I lived—when I died. What I've done and why I've done it.

I AM A TERRORIST.

But by the very people who say hexavalent chromium can't do harm when ingested—by the very governmental body that creates and enforces law—*I AM NOT A TERRORIST*
I have merely added to the water of every cooler in the United States Capitol Complex...

> [House Office Buildings]
> [Senate Office Buildings]
> [Library of Congress]
> [U.S. Capitol]
> [U.S. Supreme Court]

...concentrations of hexavalent chromium 100 times higher than the highest levels ever suffered by the people of the town of Hinckley, California for the last FIVE years.

Why?

The Environmental Protection Agency promised to study ingested hexavalent chromium (sodium dichromate) for 1 month, 3 months, 6 months, 1 year, 2 years, and 5 years but then NEVER published the findings past the 1 year study.

Now the United States politicians have all consumed hexavalent chromium. Their secretaries and their children who visit them at their office. The copy chasers. The mailroom. Everyone who's afraid to drink D.C.'s tap water but has worked in this icon of Democracy—

had better start reading what happened to those people from Hinckley. And more than that—HERE IS THE SCIENTIFIC PROOF THAT

HEXAVALENT CHROMIUM CAN CAUSE PARKINSONISM VIA . . .

"I wonder if I should have told Jamie that she'd poisoned him too," Ted asked himself.

Then he set Anne Whiting's journal down amongst the papers he was preparing for the journal abstracts that he and Dr. Rod had agreed to co-author. . .*submit present—defend*

~~~~~~~~FINALE~~~~~~~~

For a few months no one saw, or heard from, James R. Pickett and—truth be told—Jen began to worry that, perhaps, Asamu had been right about the man she'd sworn was as much in love with her as she with him.

Then one afternoon—not nearly-spring but not deeply-winter—James R. Pickett opened the door to the Gene Whiting Library for, what would prove, his last time and asked Jen Stell to join him for lunch.

They decided to try a new restaurant: a small café on the town's square with kosher meals. It was very trendy and had gotten great reviews.

At the table there were the awkward moments. . .

I wonder why he didn't even call

I hope she still feels the way she said she did

And—in unison solitudinous quiets: *My GOD, I feel. . .*

. . . until Jamie—succumbing to an emersion of his weary soul into the warmth and promises of—

. . .gave Jen an envelope.

She opened it to find the deed to the house on Granite Street with her name [Jen Stell] typed in [New Times Roman 12 pointfont]

"I don't understand."

Then he handed her two rings.

Everything had come—and gone—fully encircling the lives of being-human.

FIN

[Excerpted from Anne Whiting's Diary, pages 557-567, volume 9.]

A Declaration by a representative person of the U.S.A.

"When in the course of human events it becomes necessary for one people to dissolve the political bands which have connected them with another, and to assume wrong the powers of the earth the separate and equal station to which the laws of nature and nature's God entitle them, a decent respect to the opinions of mankind requires that they should declare the causes which impel them to the separation."

I, Anne Whiting, declare myself separate from my government because it has knowingly, and for means of profit, poisoned its people.

"We hold these truths to be self-evident, that all men are created equal, that they are endowed by their Creator with inherent and unalienable rights, that among these rights are life, liberty and the pursuit of happiness: that to secure these rights, governments are instituted among men, deriving their just powers from the consent of the governed; that whenever any form of government becomes destructive of these ends, it is the right of the people to alter or abolish it, and to institute a new government, laying its foundation on such principles, and organizing its powers in such form, as to them shall seem most likely to effect their safety and happiness."

I, Anne Whiting, declare that our government has not treated each man equally—they do not put themselves in plants and occupations where they are exposed to toxins such as hexavalent chromium (although some have been soldiers…thereby being exposed) and that this government has become unjust because it knowingly puts its people in harm's way, using its legislative power to vilify and make unsafe the very people it was created to protect and serve; I have done nothing but level the playing field by exposing these people to hexavalent chromium but they will call me a terrorist.

" Prudence indeed will dictate that governments long established should not be changed for light and transient causes; and accordingly all experience hath shown that mankind are more disposed to suffer, while evils are sufferable, than to right themselves by abolishing the forms to which they are accustomed."

I, Anne Whiting, must tell you that what I did went against my very soul; I never want to hurt anyone but the only way to make our government's officials fight their own greed was to make them want to fight more so for their very lives. Please believe me that I tried every possible way to get people to pay attention, to research: all in the hope of finally doing no harm…of protecting people, like my husband, from being poisoned by hexavalent chromium…but there was no other way.

"But when a long train of abuses and usurpations begun at a distinguished period and pursuing invariably the same object, evinces a design to reduce them under absolute despotism, it is their right, it is their duty to throw off such government, and to provide new guards for their future security."

I, Anne Whiting, feel compelled to tell you that definitive studies have proven hexavalent chromium causes cancer (educate yourselves…begin with the Industrial Revolution and smelters…end with computers, cell phones, et. al.). The information is not new but when researchers have either studied (or proposed to study) the full health effects of hexavalent chromium somehow the studies either never take place or are halted thereby providing the failsafe that there is no proof that there are any deleterious health effects via multiple exposure pathways. This is a deception that is longstanding and deliberate and the reason why I have done what I've done…there can be no more lies.

"Such has been the patient sufferance of these colonies; and such is now the necessity which constrains them to expunge their former system of government."

I, Anne Whiting, attest that hexavalent chromium poisoning causes MUCH suffering…unduly and, currently, without sympathy, empathy, or understanding because of our government's denial of its full toxicity.

"The history of the present King of Great Britain is a history of unremitting injuries and usurpations, among which appears no solitary fact to contradict the uniform tenor of the rest but all have in direct object the establishment of an absolute tyranny over these States."

I, Anne Whiting, declare that our government has a long history of industrial poisonings (by legislating such that private industry can continue to contaminate means that the legislative power is culpable) and hexavalent chromium is but one offender. The people have no one to protect us from industrialists except our legislators; legislators who create affordable penalties for poisoning such that industrialists would rather pay fines than stop poisoning the people of this great country. This is tyranny!

"To prove this, let facts be submitted to a candid world for the truth of which we pledge a faith yet unsullied by falsehood."

1. "He has refused his assent to laws, the most wholesome and necessary for the public good." [Industrial pollutants such as hexavalent chromium put the public in danger—but the laws (when enforced) do not in any way dissuade industrial pollution.]

2. "He has dissolved representative houses, repeatedly, and continually for opposing with manly firmness his invasions on the rights of the people." [When studies either have shown, or are near to showing, the full health effects of ingesting hexavalent chromium over long periods of time (5+ years) the information does not become available to the public and often times researchers are made to feel pressure in their reporting.]

3.   "He has refused for a long time, after such dissolutions, to cause others to be elected, whereby the legislative powers, incapable of annihilation, have returned to the people at large for their exercise; the State remaining in the meantime exposed to all the dangers of invasion from without, and convulsions within." [In Hudson, New Jersey, tons of hexavalent chromium were improperly managed by Honeywell, Inc. for DECADES. Health officials are still helpless to provide aide to the people due to the stalemate between the EPA and the private corporation as to who, when, how, etc. proper cleanup and provisions for health benefits for the contaminated are to ensue].

4.   "He has made our judges dependent on his will alone, for the tenure of their offices, and the amount and payment of their salaries." [Industrialists influence government…Industrialists pollute with known toxins such as hexavalent chromium yet they are allowed to continue. This implies condoning; I can only surmise, then, that it profits the government to allow Industrialists to poison its own people.]

5. "He has erected a multitude of new officers to harass our people and eat our substance." [The very departments created to protect the people from Industrial Pollution are now functioning to protect the Industrialist by dismissing—using the People's own resources against them—all claims against the Industrialists.]

6. "He has combined with others to subject us to a jurisdiction foreign to our Constitution, and unacknowledged by our laws; giving his assent to their acts of pretended legislation:...:for protecting them, by mock-trial, from punishment for any murders which they could commit on the inhabitants of these States:..." [Our Constitution is a beautiful thing. It is being violated by those who've conspired with Industrialists for profit when the cost—the cost is the People of the United States of America. The people are paying the cost...they are paying the health bills, they are suffering the loss of loved ones...they are suffering because our own legislators prefer Industrialists to the People. It is criminal! I, Anne Whiting, SHOULD go to jail for MURDER for putting hexavalent chromium in

the Government's water…just as ALL THE INDUSTRIALISTS should also be put in jail for MURDER! I wonder which ones of us will get there first…hmmm].

7.   "He is, at this time transporting large armies of foreign mercenaries to complete the works of death, desolation and tyranny, already begun with circumstances of cruelty and perfidy (scarcely paralleled in the most barbarous ages, and totally) unworthy the head of a civilized Nation." [Yet, in order that we should all be equal—all equally exposed to hexavalent chromium, not just the poor or the worker—I, Anne Whiting, will be called a criminal for poisoning the government's water with something THEY claim is not poison. I will be arrested, tried (perhaps…terrorists aren't treated the same as regular criminals…certainly not as Industrial criminals are, that's for sure) and maybe even sentenced to death…though I already am (dead that is). This is truly the mark of a barbarously unequal system. Our government has become that which we fought against two centuries ago…]

8.   "In every stage of these oppressions we have petitioned for redress in the most humble terms: our repeated petitions have been answered only by repeated injury." [I, Anne Whiting, have boxes and boxes of letters from officials, researchers, experts all saying the same thing…there is no money in researching the health effects of hexavalent chromium even though it is CURRENTLY an industry standard…IT IS EVERYWHERE and all over the world. When I've pleaded with people to study…they refused. The government turns its blind eye for Industry.]

9.   "A Prince whose character is thus marked by every act which may define a tyrant, is unfit to be the ruler of a people who mean to be free. Future ages will scarcely believe that the hardiness of one man adventured, within the short compass of twelve years only, to lay a foundation so broad and so undisguised for tyranny over a people fostered and fixed in principles of freedom." [I, Anne Whiting, know Americans want to be protected from being poisoned. We don't want our children poisoned. Our representatives and our legislators and our president

KNOW we don't want to be poisoned. Our government not only has failed to protect us…they've had a hand in POISONING us! I can scarcely believe that we, as a people, continue to allow our governors…our caretakers…to act so murderously. I can but hope…that perhaps my actions might one day be better understood for I love America more than you can know.]

10.   "We must endeavor to forget our former love for them, and hold them as we hold the rest of mankind, enemies in war, in peace friends."

11.   "We might have been a great people together; but a communication of grandeur and of freedom it seems is below their dignity."

12.   "Be it so, since they will have it. The road to happiness and to glory is open to us too."

13.   "We will tread it apart from them, and acquiesce in the necessity which denounces our eternal separation."

14.   "And for the support of this declaration (with a firm reliance on the protection of Divine Providence) we

mutually pledge to each other our lives, our fortunes, and
our sacred honor."

Quoted: The Declaration of Independence.

~~~~~~~~~~~~~Your Notes & Thoughts~~~~~~~~~~~~

www.ingramcontent.com/pod-product-compliance
Lightning Source LLC
Chambersburg PA
CBHW031948240626
47153CB00003B/906